Heidi

John Gumbs

Published by John Gumbs
Publishing partner: Paragon Publishing, Rothersthorpe
First published 2019
© John Gumbs 2019, London

ISBN 978-1-78222-682-6

Book design, layout and production management by Into Print
www.intoprint.net
+44 (0)1604 832149

Contents

1

Meeting Up With Heidi

The meeting of Heidi and I was accidental. It was as if we knew each other before - very strange it is.

I'VE BEEN PUTTING off going to the bank for a long time. Finally, I made up my mind, and decided it shall be today. I got all the papers ready that I would need to take, caught the bus going to town, and then to the bank. Half an hour later, I was out the bank and heading down in the town. A few meters away from the bank, there was a man behind a cheese stand with three customers there. I joined the queue. Why was I at the cheese stand was a mystery to me. I had no need for cheese because I hadn't eaten it for a long time now. Planning to move away, I suddenly noticed this tall blonde girl on my right. Her hair was short, and if it had been singed. She had on some brown boots, and it seemed to me that they were too big for her. She wore a nice green long summer dress. Her bicycle was beside her with a bag on either side of the back wheel. She got served and moved away, the same time as I moved away. We bumped into each other.

She said, "Pardon."

I said, "No, no. It's my fault. I'm the one who should be saying 'pardon.'" She got onto her bike. There was a smile on her face. I started trotting beside her.

"Never seen you in town before? Are you new here?"

"No." She answered.

"Are you married?" I had to ask that. It was very important to me to find out.

"I live apart from my husband," she said

"Do you still see each other?"

"Why all these questions? She asked.

"I'm interested in you, that's why!"

"But you only saw me a minute ago!"

"I know, can't help it." I said to her.

"Now and again we bump into each other." She told me

"I was thinking if you have time, what about a quick coffee? Would you like that?"

She was having trouble making up her mind to do so or not.

"I'm not going to eat you," I said. "And you don't need to be afraid."

"Okay, then," she said. "Ten minutes."

Just a few meters away was a coffee place. We went and found a table with chairs. She had parked her bike against the railing. Sitting down, I ordered coffee.

"Nothing like a good hot fresh cup of coffee around this time." I told her. "By the way, I'm John and you?!"

"My name is Heidi!"

"That's a nice name, like Heidi from the TV show."

"I have to be going now," she said. "Thanks for the coffee!"

"Can we meet again?" I asked her

"Maybe. Can't say yet. See you!"

"So long Heidi! See you again!" I said as she rode off.

I began to think how lucky I was to bump into her that way. My luck must be in, but I still have to be careful. She was only parted from her husband - both living separately. The chance is always there for them to get back together. Still, it was a great thing to meet her even though I don't mess about with married women, or with those who are courting.

A whole week passed by and I saw her again. She was on her bicycle as usual riding through the market. She did not see me. I called out "Heidi!"

She stopped, look back over her left shoulder, and spotted me. Arriving where she was, she said, "Hi, nice to see you again. How was your week?"

"It went by quickly," I told her. "And you? How's everything?"

"Oh! So and so. But I'm getting along."

I walked round with her as she picked up her groceries and bits and pieces. We had a coffee, chatted, and then she was on her way home.

The next time I met up with her, I asked her if she would like to go bicycling. She said that would be great. I was planning to take her across the bridge, then 100 meters on the right, there was a road leading up to an old castle, but not habited. Down by the riverside there was a nice sandy spot where we could have a picnic. I told her all about it, and she liked the idea.

Together, on a day, nice and sunny, we rode up to the castle, then took a track down to the riverside. There, we set up for picnic. I noticed as we had turned right, just in front the castle, there was a sign on its left side, but I couldn't make out clearly what it said. Half of the solid door - the right half was open - inwards.

An hour passed by as we sat there looking at the bridge spanning across the water. Not far from us was another couple, the woman in swim suit, the man in swim shorts.

"I have to go to the WC," Heidi said to me. "I'll go to that castle. I see the door is half open."

She got up and went up to the castle. An hour passed

by and still there was no sign of her. I left everything there where it was, and walked up to the castle. Inside the door I had to turn right for there was a fancy worked partition blocking the way. On my left, there were stairs leading up. A door right was half open, and I could see a gaping big hole there. In the corner on my right was a small door, opening it, I saw small winding steps. I went down and found myself in a long corridor. I started walking along it, calling out her name. Half an hour later, I found myself by a walled circular space with a small door. I opened the door, and there were winding steps going upwards. There was lots of noise, and a strange shaking as if everything was going to collapse. Taking the stairs upwards, I came to a circular top. At the foot of this circular foundation, I saw on the left a small entrance with an iron rail around it. It wasn't fastened but on two hinges. I opened and peeped in. There were small steps leading down. I was now wondering had she come this far? Had she taken this route? The place was dark, cold and smelly, and at times I felt short of breath.

I went down the stairs which were very steep, then at the bottom, a sharp right to the side of the circular pillar I just came from. There was just enough room for two people side by side to walk along. The next tunnel was very long and broad. It took a while before I had to turn left. I realised too, that I was very deep down. And if I was right, underneath the water of the bridge. I kept calling out but no answer.

It wasn't far from another flight of stairs upwards that I found her crouching there, not herself at all. Light was filtering through, and I heard voices up above the steps. I held her tightly and told her that she'll be alright. Help is at hand. Then the firemen were there, with the ambulance and policemen and the newspaper men.

The people who were at the riverside, below us, must have known something was wrong when they hadn't seen us come back, and the bicycles and picnic basket still there, and called for help.

An iron grilled door was moved, and men came and rescued us It was a clever thing those builders did with the tunnel. It came from the castle, came down to the nearest end of the bridge, crossing the river, then it went right down to the old crossing from Lent deep under the water, then up to this iron grill door we came through.. She was lucky that she was wearing jeans that day. She only ended up with a couple of scratches.

Outside the tunnel I had to put my hand across my face to stop some flashing that was going on. The medic checked us over and we were okay. Walking back across the bridge, and up the road to the castle, I said to her, "You were very brave to be in that tunnel, and it was rather deep."

'She said, "I got the fright of my life when I opened that door in the castle and found myself on the floor below, with winding stairs going somewhere."

"What did you do?"

"I couldn't do much," she said. "There was no one around."

As we came to the castle, to go on the track down to the riverside and to where our bicycles were, I remembered when we first came up, there was a sign on the left side of the building. It said: 'No entrance.' Of course, none of us had read it. We got to the place where our bikes were, and the picnic area, packed up and rode away. It so happened that when we came back down the road from the castle, she wasn't living far away from where we were. There was another thing, she knew about the castle, but not of the tunnels beneath it.

We met again for coffee, and chatted over that strange dangerous incident. The next day after that dreadful event, it was in the front news. "Man and woman found in secret tunnels'. Looking at the paper that was on the table, she said, "How strange life is really! If I hadn't met you, I would not have been through that tunnel."

I said to her, "There was a sign saying not to enter the castle. I found out later, that there were workmen upstairs on the third floor working. It was careless of them to have left the entrance to the tunnel with only a carpet over it."

"It was the carpet that broke my fall. At the bottom I shouted my head off and no one came. I must say though that the tunnel was very clean, only it was cold smelly and damp."

"But why did you leave the entrance and wandered away? You should have stayed where you were."

"You saw it for yourself that there was a shoot stretching straight and slanting down. That's why I didn't hurt myself. At the bottom, I saw those winding stairs, and I took them."

"Do you know that the bridge cost a lot of money to build; and was then blown up to prevent the Germans from crossing over. They still crossed over in rubber boats."

"That was a horrible time with lots of confusion," she said to me. "I hope nothing like that ever happen again!"

"I know what you mean," I said. "We have no say in such happenings. But that bridge, I love it. I like the way those engineers constructed it, and when I'm on top of it and walking along, there's a great feeling flowing through me, and the scenery is great."

"I'm with you on that one," she said. "It is pleasurable riding along it. Coming from Lent, I take the bicycle track along the rail bridge, down along the path by where the old ferry transport came, from Nijmegen, then I ride up onto the bridge."

"Every time I come down to the town, I always feel like going for a walk along the same route."

"That's amazing!" She said, and she smiled.

"Yes, the attraction of the place cause me to have that feeling." I told her.

2

The House In The Woods

I managed to get Heidi to go away for two weeks to the house in the woods.

THE TIME CAME when Heidi had to leave again. Getting on her bicycle she told me that next time we meet, we'll take the route I told her about. "That should be pleasant," she said. She left, and I went looking around the town.

Nijmegen is a large city in Gelderland, and the eldest in the Netherlands. It has a large student population. Its history goes back some 2000 years - Roman times. It was called Noviomagus. There was a Roman settlement which got destroyed by fire, a later settlement was built up with the name Noviomagus, this means 'New Market'.

We met again and took a route along the riverside, then up the many steps up to the bicycle and pedestrian lane, alongside the rail line. After a while, we turn to our right, down more steps, and along the road where a few houses stood. Just behind them was the place where the ferry from Lent to Nijmegen used to run. Looking across the water to Nijmegen,

I said, "Just think many years ago, Nijmegen was surrounded by foreign troops. The water there, was filled with boats carrying soldiers, some to their deaths, others to safety.

"I heard it was terrible. Many soldiers got killed. War is terrible. I just don't like it." She told me.

"I know how you feel," I told her. "War is also not for me,

but there's nothing one can do when one is dragged into it."

She said, "My parents told me all about it. The Germans tricked us, having us to believe that we were neutral, then suddenly, in the early hours of the morning on 10th May 1940, there were planes all over the skies."

I said to her, "I knew a man who was married with 6 daughters, and I visited him quite often. He told me a lot about the war. And you know what? One Sunday I was walking through the park, then I went over to the side where you can see clearly, beautiful view. This guy came along, and started giving me a history about the bridge."

"If you're talking about the first bridge," she told me, "it was in 1936 when they opened it. There were over 200,000 people at the ceremony. Later, sad to say, they had to blow it up."

"Again, I say, that's war, and anything can happen." I told her.

"I'm glad I wasn't around to see all that horrible stuff, and I say praise to our soldiers who stood up so brave fighting against the enemy."

"Yes, they did a great job. I know you don't like this subject of war, so let's talk about traveling," I said. "Maybe I can take you through the woods to a house that you would really like. Long walks with your dog, and there's a swimming pool nearby."

"Where is that? She asked. "I'm interested."

I said, "It's not very far from here, and I know for sure you'd like it. We can go when you're free."

"That's fine, I'm looking forward to that. How'd you know I'd like it, and you don't know me very long?"

"I just got that feeling, it's the right feeling isn't it?" I asked.

"Of course," she said.

Two months later, we were walking up to the house in the woods. As soon as Heidi saw it, she liked it; also the surrounding area. There were many routes one could take. She said to me, "You've picked a good place, I like it."

"I'm glad you do. Hope you find it enjoyable." I told her. I opened the front door and showed her in. She was amazed at how clean the place was, and so cosy too. We sorted things out, putting them into place, had a coffee, then went for a long walk.

Walking along the dirt track in the woods, Heidi's dog went into the woods, and came back sniffing, and shaking its head. I thought that was strange and followed it as it went back in the second time. I said to her, "Stay here on the track, I shall go and take a look. The dog was on the left of me, as I went through the woods. Then I came to the spot and saw the horrible sight. There were ants crawling all over the place, with flies all around. I picked up a dry stick and used it to see what was lying there. As I pulled away what looked like a dirty white towel, I couldn't believe what I was seeing. It was a newly born babe there being eaten by those ants. I threw down the stick, grabbed the babe, still wrapped in the dirty towel, not thinking about all the ants that came upon me, and rushed out the woods, quickly reaching the track where Heidi was. I turned sharply to my right and began to run to the house. Heidi was behind me asking what's wrong? What have you got there? I was choked up and words failed me at that moment. Inside the house I immediately dialled a doctor I knew was nearby for them to come have a look at the babe. I told them the whole story. The babe's flesh was eaten here and there, and it was lucky the ants didn't get into its eyes. It was in a terrible state, and so was Heidi when she knew what it was all about.

The ambulance arrived and took the babe away, it was a boy. I had already cleaned it up as much as I could, using Dettol.

We went away with the ambulance and stayed at the hospital until late in the morning.. Back at the house in the woods, we sat down over a hot cup of coffee. It was getting on for 3:30 am. Heidi said to me, "It is horrible that a woman could do that to her new born babe. She has no feelings in her. I wonder what drove her to do such a thing?"

I said, "Maybe she was a young girl who got pregnant and didn't really want the child. That happens quite often."

"Later on today we shall pop back and see how the babe is getting on." Heidi said. "I'm ready to rest my head."

"Me too," I said. "It has been a very strange day."

A whole year went by and no one came forward to claim the babe. Notice of it had been placed in the local papers. Later, Heidi and I went through a process where we became the adopted parents. She was very pleased about it and couldn't wait to bring the babe home. Seeing that it was a boy we started looking for names. We both loved the name of Michael. He was in good shape, with only a few minor scars, barely to be seen. We brought Michael up, and made sure he had a good education.

At the age of five we picked a nice school for Michael. It wasn't far away. He had to walk a bit, and then take the bus. Both of us accompanied him and the teacher met us at the gate, and took charge of Michael. This was his first day at school, he waved to us as he went away. We were proud parents.

Walking away from the school gates, I said to Heidi, "How are you feeling. You've rescued Michael, and now you've brought him to receive education."

"You were the one who rescued him. Actually, it was the dog. If we hadn't had the dog with us, we would not have known that he was there."

I said, "That's true, the dog is the rescuer."

We were there at the end of the school day to pick up Michael. There was a big smile on his face when he saw us. Heidi took his hand. "Did you like your school?" She asked him.

"Yes mammy," he replied. "I like teacher."

"That's good ," I said, "if you like your teacher, you'll get on well."

In the papers they were still asking for the parents of Michael. No one came forward. Heidi and I decided to go to the mountain now that Michael had turned five. We got a place where we could stay for two weeks. Everyone enjoyed the holidays. On the other side of us there was a mountain quake but no one was harmed. Safely back home now, we started to teach Michael the way of life. We educated him in every way. It all went in and he was very happy. One day he came and told us a story about ants, he didn't like them. We told him no one really like them, but they are a part of the way of life on earth, just like we are a part. A month later, we were at the swimming pool when this woman came up and started hugging Michael around the neck, and calling him 'sweety.'

Heidi went over and asked, "Excuse me, do you know this child?"

"Who are you?" The woman replied.

Heidi said, "I happen to be the mother of this child!"

The woman said, "You have a nice son. Make sure you look after him." Then she went away. I could have run after her and ask her many questions, but I held myself back. Heidi said to me, "That woman is strange!"

"Do you think she could be the mother?" I asked her.

"I don't think so," she replied. "She's not the type to abandon children. But she's strange. What if the real mother comes and barging into our lives?"

I said to her, "Don't worry much about that. He is legally our son now. The real parents cannot get him back. We have a strong case in the way he was abandoned."

"I really don't understand what get into those women to go and do the things that they do, especially with new born children."

"They're not like you," I said, "who really care about humanity. Some of them are far too young to have children."

"Could you imagine around the world, how many young girls are in that situation?" Heidi said.

"There are quite a lot," I replied. And most of them have had talks from their parents or some other organization."

Heidi said, "If I ever meet the mother of Michael, I'll really tell her off."

"Some of them," I said, "don't care, they won't listen. You'll be spilling your words."

"I know, but they'll still hear it from me whether they like it or not. If they don't want to have a child, then they shouldn't get themselves pregnant."

"But that's the way those young kids are, it doesn't really matter to them," I said. "You're right, but don't get yourself in no unnecessary trouble."

"I won't," she said. "I'll just say what's on my mind, and that's that."

3

The Disappearance of Michael

Michael left home to go and catch the bus, he didn't turn up at his school.

MICHAEL REACHED THE age of ten, and was now accustomed to walk from home to the bus stop which wasn't that far away. There was a great storm the night before, the following day it was calm. We got a call that day from school reporting to us that Michael hadn't turned up at school. We told them that he left at the usual time as always.

The police department was notified, but there was nothing they could do. It was too early to make it an emergency. They'll list him as missing. He could have run away, they said. Or gone to some relatives. We had to make it clear to them what child Michael was.

Searching the area with many groups we found nothing. It still remained a mystery to us where he could be. One whole week passed by, and still no word as to where he could be located. The police kept on investigating, nothing turned up. There were posters with his picture on it all over the place, and in every town, village and city. We got news that he was seen in certain places, but they were untrue. Then some good news came that he was seen in a place about 62 kilometres from where we were.

I said to Heidi, "I'll go up and check, and let you know what's going on."

"Okay," she said.

Heidi was very much disturbed over what had happened, but remained strong. I told her many times not to get too upset, things would work out okay.

I took an early morning train up to the place where Michael was last seen. it was a long distance away, and someone must have driven him there, probably relatives from the mother or father. I spent a couple of days looking around and asking questions. Walking back to catch the train, I walked over a humped bridge, then near to the water's edge, and along a pedestrian path. There was a supermarket on the right side, with some men working on the road leading to it. I was amazed when I saw a red car pulled into the park, and a man and a woman got out holding the hand of a boy. From where I was, it was hard to tell who the boy was. I watched as they went through the door of the supermarket. With a burst of speed, I hurried across the path, into the park, then casually walked into the supermarket. It was big, and I looked around a bit until my eyes caught up with the man, the woman, and the boy. The boy was Michael

I pretended I was shopping for something, looking at the things on the shelf, and still making sure to keep that family in my sight. The boy was holding on to the trolley, and looking back now and then. He spotted me and gave a smile. I was thinking then, he probably knew who I was. Into the queue for the cashier, I noticed something odd. They were just ahead of me. The boy looked the split image of Michael, and I now was a bit hesitant. I had already phoned the local police, and told them where I was. As soon as the family left that cashier, and was outside, they were approached by the policemen who started talking to them. I came over closer and was shocked to find that the boy was not Michael at all. He had features like him. I then had to explain myself to the policemen and the family. They all agreed, and saw from the posters, that the boy looked somewhat like Michael.

I phoned Heidi and told her all that had happened, and that I'm on my way back. "That was an awful experience for you, having called the police, you were sure that the boy was Michael." Heidi said.

"It was a bit awkward at the time. Now it's all behind me, and we have to move forward." I told her. "Our aim is, get our son back no matter what."

She made me a cup of coffee, and I said to her, "You see that farm that is 6 kilometres from the bus stop where Michael went missing, I'm going to snoop around there to see what I can pick up. They have already been cleared by the police, and special investigators."

"What! Do you think they could have something to do with it?" She asked.

"I don't know, but I have to find out."

It was one of those farms, open all around. As soon as they saw me they came out, and greeted me. Over in the fields, I saw the cows and horses. There were no dogs. I found that pretty unusual. I think its possible to find some farms like this one. A fair size farm, it was. I stayed an hour and a half chatting with the owner and his wife. They told me that they hadn't seen any strange people around, only the farm hands. They had already told the police what they know.

From the farm I met up with Heidi, and we went out shopping. I enjoy going shopping, whether on my own or with someone. With a woman you have to be patient, be still, and follow around everywhere, of course you can make conversation, but be careful not to upset her. It is an experience going shopping with your wife or your girlfriend. They take hours and finally comes out with one item, a dress or a pair of shoes. I'm not here talking about shopping for food, that is something different but still can be an experience for you. Heidi wasn't like that, of course she'll look around, but didn't take hours to find what she wanted.

We headed back home. She said to me, "Something has to turn up sooner than later. Where do you think Michael could be?"

"I have the strong feeling that he's safe.," I told her. "I don't think any harm will come to him."

Heidi had gone on a day to visit her parents. I had the dog in care. She phoned and said she was on her way back. She came off the bus, crossed over a few streets, and as she was walking down a lane boarded on both sides, she picked up the sound of kids playing. Stopping and keeping her ear alert, she heard the voice of Michael. There was a house on her left and also one on her right. Going closer to the fence, she peeped through a crack, but it was hard to see through all the trees that were in the garden. A gate was there, about a few metres from where she was. As she turned to go to the gate, this big guy with his head like a bull dog grabbed her, and tugged her in the gate. I was on my way with the dog to meet her. It was around 19:30. The dog knew something was wrong, and started tugging away. I followed. It brought me to the alley way, and the gate. I knew now that something was dreadfully wrong. Taking my mobile, I phoned the police. I went through the gate, only to get a great whack across my shoulder, it really hurt. I went down in pain. I saw the dog holding fast to the guy's right leg and wouldn't let go. I got up and went into him as hard as I could, but I knew it wasn't going to hurt him none. Every time he kicked the dog away, it came back, and would not give up.

I remembered when I was in the Army, I used to go and watch the rugby players train. One day I saw how this small bloke tackled another guy twice the size of himself, and had him there on the ground. Immediately I got the courage, using some foot work, and my shoulder, I went into him again, this time sending him crashing to the ground. If I had missed, I would have been in much trouble. The police was there on the scene, and arrested the guy.

Looking around this house and its surroundings was strange.. It was rather difficult to get to the house. But when we did so, there was a middle-aged woman, she immediately show where Heidi was. At the left side of the house, there were stairs leading down to a cellar. We found five children there, three boys and two girls; among them was Michael. He was glad to see us. We hugged him and took him away. The dog, later, we took to the vet. It had some foot injuries, and a cut just to the side of its mouth.

A week later, we took Michael out on a day trip to a big amusement park. You could see he was enjoying every minute of it. He had already told us what had happened on that day at the bus stop. We had warned him not to go with strangers, and to be careful. He told us that the car came along with a woman driving, and a man beside her along with some children. They told him that the bus wasn't coming for there was a strike on, and that they would take him to the school. Seeing the other children, he accepted, and went with them. On the day Michael left home for school, we had already checked that the bus was running. We all enjoyed ourselves at the amusement park, and it was late when we got back home. Michael went straight to bed, he was very tired. Heidi and I stayed up a bit, and then we too, went to bed.

4

Michael has turned twelve years old

This is the year that Michael had a fantastic birthday, but then afterwards some strange things happened.

MICHAEL HAD A fantastic birthday when he was aged 12. He enjoyed all his birthdays, but this one was special. This was the year that things started going wrong in his class in the school.

For no reason whatsoever, the whole floor of the classroom was filled with ants. All the other children had to get out the class as quick as possible, and there were phone calls to us. Heidi was at home at the time. She had to go in and see what it was all about. The health team was already there and cleaning up. Heidi had to explain to the teacher what she think was happening. We already know how we found him, but that doesn't explain the situation now. The doctors couldn't do anything to help.

I said to Heidi, "I think the time has come to tell Michael about how we found him, covered in ants."

"That might scare him a bit," she said. "Do we have to tell him?"

"We have to tell him sometime. He is old enough to understand."

"I's a delicate subject, and we must be careful what we tell him. How is he going to take it? It must be told to him in a good way, and not to disturb him," she told me. "He's going to ask many questions, and we have to be prepared to answer them. Some children comes out of it, and carry on living a good normal life."

"Michael is intelligent, lovable, and is at the age to know good from bad. We know that he doesn't like ants, and that episode in the school was just ridiculous. Let's hope that he doesn't think of it too hard. At least there was no harm done to him or anyone in the school."

Heidi said, "We'll ease him into a chat, see how he's feeling, and then maybe, well, you never know."

"Do you think that there's something magical about him?" I asked her.

"We haven't seen anything in that area. He's a nice decent boy. I don't know how to explain the ants. That in itself could be magical, but it doesn't happen often."

"I could tell him about how we found him, but that could spark off a fuse. He could make a big fuss wanting to find out who they are, and then want to meet them. We don't even know who they are?"

"So you think we should not tell him anything?" She asked.

"Michael loves us, you know that, and he's happy with us. I personally think we should keep it that way. Let him grow up and have a family of his own."

"We keep our mouths shut, not a word to him, you agree?" Heidi asked.

"Yes, I agree. We are his parents. We should be a solid force together." I told her.

"That's what we are, and we will keep it that way. Tomorrow we'll talk to him." Heidi said.

Michael had joined an outdoor group, and on the day he came back home, we got him in the living room. I said to him, "Michael, do you love your parents?"

"Of course, I do," he answered. "Why did you ask?"

"There are some children who do not like their parents." I said.

"Well, I do, and you know that. You're good parents to me."

Heidi asked, "So you're really happy that we're your parents?"

"Very happy, I am. You're the best parents. I'm not jealous of anyone else, I love you both."

I was satisfied that he felt good with us, and there was no reason now to bring the ants into the conversation. I avoided talking about them. Heidi asked him, "This outdoor group that you're in, are you happy with it?" He said he was and was having a great time.

"Soon," I said, "you'll be going away for two weeks. Take the necessary things that you need, and look after yourself."

"I will," he told us.

The chat with Michael went okay. There were no misunderstanding between us. As parents he loved us and was happy. The time for summer camp came and he went away with the outdoor group he had joined.. One and a half weeks later, the news came to us that Michael was missing. He was in a tent with two other youngsters, and suddenly, the ants were everywhere. Michael and the youngsters fled out the tent. From that moment on they hadn't seen him.

Rescue teams were out, helicopters were overhead, and yet, there was no Michael. The news hit us hard, we hadn't expected anything like this. I decided to go out to the camp area, and look around. Heidi decided to come with me as well. I told her that it could be dangerous, but she didn't mind. I was told I'd be lucky if I found him because the teams had been through the area thoroughly.

I was wondering why did Michael ran away? Why didn't he stay with the rest, and get help? There must be some other explanation. Getting all the details of the area was easy. Heidi and I took lots of things that we know we would need, and we were off.

We got up the first steep slope and Heidi was shattered. "I told you it would be hard." I said to her.

"I know. I know. Let me have a rest, then we can go on." She said, out of breath.

Taking a ten minute break, we had some water and was ready to take the next stage.. We got to the top and found ourselves on a flattened piece of ground. On the right about 200 metres, was a rope bridge going across a stretch of water. I hate these rope bridges. You're left dangling in the middle, trying to keep your balance, and being careful where you put your feet. At least, the planks were joined continuously, but at either side, there was a gaping hole all along where the ropes joined to the planks.

Heidi had brought her dog along, and it was shaking as it took steps along. I was in front, and Heidi was just behind me. If anything goes wrong, I had the emergencies' numbers, and could just give them a call. I was just about to tell Heidi to watch her footing, when her left foot accidentally left the plank and took the gaping hole on her left side. She stumbled down grabbing with both hands on the rope, and sending the bridge swinging. The dog was just behind her in the middle on the planks. I got her safely out of that hole, luckily there was no damage done to her.

Safely back in the middle of the bridge, on the wooden planks, she said, "You had warned me that it would be dangerous. And now I see it for myself."

I said, "Not far to go now. We just got to get to the end of the bridge, a few metres through the wood, and then we are there."

Getting off the rope bridge was a relief. Even the dog showed it. Heidi was okay and ready for the rest of the journey.

Through a thick forest we went and came out into an opening which was where Michael and the rest had camped. I looked at my map and my notes, and we were in the right place.

Repeatedly, we called Michael's name but got no response. At the place where Michael's group had camped, we set up camp. Later in the day, the dog was sniffing around. "Is she onto something?" I asked.

"She's very sensitive, and will easily pick up the track of Michael." She told me.

"That's what dogs do." I told her.

"Come have a look at this," Heidi said. "It's a massive ants nest just at the beginning of the woods."

I went over and had a look. It was really big and spreading out, the dog would go near, and then pull back quickly. I noticed something strange, as if I saw some one. I said to Heidi, "Did you see what I saw?"

"You mean a sort of swift movement,? Yes, I did!"

Taking a closer look, I suddenly saw the shape became clearer, and then there was Michael facing us. The dog barked a few times, then was still. "Michael, Michael," I said. "What's going on. How did you do what you just did?"

Heidi herself was amazed. She had never seen anything like that before. She couldn't believe that she was seeing what she had seen. We were all surprised and glad at the same time. Michael was safe and well, and that was the most vital thing, that is why we were here to find him. We had been told that we had no chance of finding him, because the rescue teams had done their jobs thoroughly. Walking over to where we were staying, I said to Michael, "There's a lot more you have to explain to us. Have you got some sort of unseen powers that you don't want us to know about? We'll keep our mouths shut."

We had drinks and were seated, Michael said, "I'm an ant,

and I have the power to change into a human being. You have just seen for yourselves that it is so."

Heidi said, "When did you first realize that you had this power?"

Michael answered, "It was always with me. I tried it out a few times, and it actually worked. I wanted to tell you both the news, but I held back."

"We don't mind at all that you have this power, you're still our son, and we shall look after you as long as we're alive." I told him.

Heidi said, "Then you must have changed into an ant when you rushed out the tent. That's why they couldn't find you?"

Michael said, "Yes, into a male ant, I had wings, could fly."

"Go on, tell us more," I said. "Sounds interesting."

"It is, but as a male ant, there's not much to do. We are there only to serve the queen, to mate with her." Michael told us.

Heidi said, "Did you..."

"Yes, as a male ant, I had no choice. The queen carries on laying eggs, and making sure that there are many workers. We are very social and look after each other. The workers keep on building, so we spread and become a great colony. Don't you find it strange that I don't like ants, and yet, I've turned into one? I don't like the idea of dying as soon as you've mated. The queen lives to be about 9 years. It take us about 3 months to become an adult."

"This experience of yours," I told him, "is fantastic. Not many people are going to believe it."

"I wouldn't like to be there permanent. As I told you, the male ant die quickly. I'd rather be like I am now" Michael told us.

Heidi said, "You're safe and sound, and we're going to take you home."

We took Michael back with us across that rope bridge, every one got across safely.

5

Michael's real Parents

*We got a shock, a real shock when the father of Michael
turned up.*

WE WERE JUST about to settle down for lunch when the door-
bell rang. I got up from the table, and went to see who it was. I
opened the door, and there facing me on the steps was a young
man around 30. "Yes," I said. The young man said, "My name is
Edward, and I've come to see my son."

I got a shock because I wasn't expecting the parents of
Michael at any time. Heidi and Michael were behind me.
She showed herself next to me, while Michael stayed hidden.
"What does he want?" Heidi asked.

I said, "I'll see to it, tell you later."

I turn to Edward and said, "We're just about to have lunch
you don't mind coming back in an hour's time, do you?"

"Oh, no," he said. "That's okay. I'll come back later." Then he
went away. I was glad Michael didn't hear what he said at the
very beginning. Peeping behind Heidi, Michael had already
had a glimpse of the features of the man on the steps. He knew
that he himself looked just like the man.

Back inside at the table and eating, Heidi said, "He's coming
back, that man. What is he after? What does he want?"

"Something to do with finances," I told her. At the same
time I was giving her a wink towards Michael, and she caught
on quickly. Michael was busy eating his lunch, and we thought

he didn't know what was happening, we were wrong, he knew. In fact he knew quite a lot. After lunch, and going up to do some study, he said, "I know that you're not my real parents, but I still love you both, wouldn't trade you in for gold." And with that he was off upstairs.

"Heidi said, "We don't have to worry now about not telling him about his real parents. He knows the truth, and there's nothing we can do. Do you think he knows how he was found?"

"I don't think so," I told her. "But with his powers, one never know."

"This man Edward," Heidi said, "when he comes back, we'll have to tell him all about Michael."

"We've got no choice," I said. "Maybe not everything if you know what I mean."

Edward came on time and I let him in. He shook hands with Heidi, then sat on the sofa. He said, "Sorry to come to you like this but I had to. I just want to see my son."

We asked him if he wanted a drink, he said yes, and we gave him a soft drink. "Tell us," I said to him, "about the history of your son."

"I was 18," he said, "and my girl was 15."

"That's pretty young!" Heidi said.

"Yeah, I know, but we were in love, and suddenly she found herself pregnant. She broke up with me and had the baby on her own. It was only later that I found out about this."

"But how did you know that we had him?" I asked.

"I checked around," he said, "and got to know that you adopted him. I don't want to take him away from you or nothing like that."

"I'm afraid that's not possible to take him away from us. Under law, we're his lawful parents now." Heidi told him.

I said to him, "you're the split image of him. Is there anything else you can tell us about him?"

Heidi looked at me.

"Only that he is living with you," Edward said. Just then, Michael came from upstairs where he had been studying.

At first everyone was silent for a minute, then Edward said, "Son, come let me hug you, it's been a long time." He got up and took Michael in his arms, hugged him. I could feel the tears springing into my eyes. "Where's my real mum? Michael asked.

"She'll be coming around soon to see you as well. She misses you very much."

I was about to say something, but I held back.

Heidi said, "She only has to give us a call to let us know when she's coming."

Edward said to Michael, "You have grown up and doing so well. I'm really proud of you."

I said, "Michael is a good boy, and he'll be doing well in later life. We try to teach him everything that we know is good. He takes it in well."

"He's doing better than me, I'm just a normal worker with no good great education. Both of you have done a great job. His mother will be very pleased."

I could see that Heidi wanted to ask something too, and she was holding back. I finally asked Edward, "Are you in a relationship now?"

"I've been in a relationship now for five years. Glad you ask that because I was hoping you'd let us have Michael for a week."

Heidi asked, "Your mate, does she like children?"

Edward said, "She's mad about them. They mean a lot to her."

"Michael," I said, "do you like the idea of spending a week with your real father?"

Michael said, "No problem. If he doesn't treat me well, I'll come back to you."

Heidi started to say, "There's something.."

I said quickly to Edward, "That's settled then. Just let us know which week."

After Edward left, and Michael was out in the garden, I said to Heidi, "I think we should not tell him about Michael's powers. And I think also we should not tell him about how we found Michael. He knows nothing about it. Let's leave it just as it is."

Heidi said, "Suppose Michael change while he's there with him, he'll then know that Michael is different than other boys."

I said, "It took much longer than a week for anything like that to overtake him. It only happens in a long while. We need not worry much about that."

"We could have flatly refused to have the mother to come and see Michael." Heidi told me. "She doesn't deserve to be next to him after what she has done. She's definitely not a good mother. Lucky is she that we don't make a big fuss out of it. I will tell her off when I see her."

"Just be careful," I said.

The week that Michael went away with his father Edward, was the same week that Melinda came to us. She was a short woman around 25, and there wasn't anything really attracted about her. Heidi just didn't take to her at all. Inside the house we sat down and started talking.

Heidi said, "So you're the mother of Michael?"

Melinda answered, "Yes, I am. Is Michael around?"

I said, "No, he's away for a week with his father."

Her face changed and she said, "Oh, I see."

Heidi said to Melinda, "What was going through your head when you abandon Michael?"

"I didn't come here to talk about that, and it's none of your business. That's all behind me now."

"Maybe so, but you abandon him, and we're his parents now. We'll take care of him." Heidi told her.

Melinda said, "Have you ever been through the pain of child birth? You don't know what it's like, do you? Only when you've been through it, then you can talk."

I said to Melinda, I don't think we'll let you have Michael. You haven't proven yourself to be a good mother. Sorry, it has to be like that."

"Are you saying his own mother cannot see him?"

"That's what I just said."

Heidi said, "Well, I think we have nothing more to say. If you had shown yourself to be a good mother, then it would have been different, sorry."

Melinda left us with an angry face.

"She has a cheek really to come here, and show her face, after what she's done to Michael," I said. "Good riddance of her, hope we don't see her again."

"I still can't understand how some women can do what she did." Heidi said. "It's a terrible shame."

I started feeling sorry. "Do you think we were too hard on her?"

Heidi said, "Not at all. That will teach her a lesson, and all the others as well, who behaved like she did."

Edward came back with Michael, and I was pleased to hear that Michael had a good time. Edward made arrangements to take Michael again at another time, and we agreed to it. Two days later, I was in the kitchen giving Heidi a helping hand. Michael was outside in the garden. Looking through the window I suddenly see Michael disappear. Putting the towel that I had in my hand aside, I said to Heidi, "He's done it again!"

"Who? What you're talking about?" She said.

"Michael has disappeared." I told her. "Don't panic, I know how to find him." We went outside, and started looking around for an ants nest. There was a small one just by the fence. "Okay, Michael, we're here. You can come back now!" Nothing happened. We called his name many times, all but to no avail. I said, "Maybe he's gone for good this time. If he go mating with the queen, that's it, we won't see him again."

Heidi said, "I hope he'll remember, and don't do that. Then he has the chance to come back."

A whole week passed, and still no sign of Michael. We must now admit that we missed him very much. He is our adopted son, and we loved him as if he was our real son. We want him back, but this strange power for now, was against us..

Heidi said, "I'm glad it didn't happen when he was with Edward. That would have been terrible. We hadn't told him about the powers Michael has. He probably would have panic, not knowing what to do, and would have called in the emergency people. But we know how to handle the situation."

"Let's just wait," I said, he'll come back."

"What if he doesn't? Heidi said. "We can't turn ourselves into ants and go to check."

"He'll come back," I told her.

Another week passed and still no sign of Michael.

"I get the feeling that this is it," Heidi said. "No more Michael. Our time with him has ended."

"Stay positive," I told her. "He's our son, and he'll not abandon us like that."

"But you know anything could happen with his powers. Within the ant community, it could be the end of him. And we won't see him any more. I'm not sleeping well, lately. Thinking too much about him."

Michael appeared at the ant nest just at the edge of the garden. Heidi and myself were in the kitchen. The door opened, and we both got up when we saw Michael. We hugged him, sat back down and listened to his story. "I bet you two were worried! I said earlier that I preferred to stay here always, but the power has control over me, I cannot do anything about it. Again, I avoided mating, and so avoided the dying process."

Heidi said, "We're glad that you're back and safe. And we understand about your powers."

6

The Humiliation Of Heidi

The brother of Melinda, Bertram, decided to do something to Heidi when he heard how she had spoken to his sister.

MELINDA GOT BACK, phoned her brother Bertram, and told him how Heidi had treated her. Bertram was a big sturdy fellow, he told his sister that he would deal with it later after she had given him the address where Heidi live. The day that Bertram came to the house, I was in the town, and Michael was away in the woods with the dog. Heidi was home alone busy cooking. Bertram let himself through the gate and went up to the house. He knocked on the door, Heidi came, opened it, but it was too late to stop the big man. He pushed the door aside half-knocking Heidi down, stepped in and closed the door behind him. Heidi managed to say, "Who are you? What do you want?"

The man grabbed her up, looked deep in her eyes and said, "I'm here to pay you back for what you said to my sister. No one talk to any of my family like that.

The man took Heidi to the kitchen, saw the mobile there, and took it up. Then he took her to the living room. "Where's your man?"

"He's away shopping. He could be back any minute!"

"And the boy?"

"He's away in the woods. I want you to let me go and get out my house." Heidi said to the man.

It was late afternoon, and Bertram tied Heidi up and gagged her, stop her from screaming. Hurriedly he took her to his car and drove away.

I had been phoning Heidi many times and got no reply. To me, this was unusual, so I tried to get back as quick as possible. It took just about half hour for me to get back home, only to find the front door wide open, and the gate ajar. Taking my mobile, I phoned the police and told them that something was wrong. I gave them all the details of how I found the place. Not long after, Michael turned up with the dog. He told me that the dog was pulling him all the time to go back home. I said, "Yes, her dog is very sensitive."

"Where is mama?" Michael asked. I told him that I didn't know myself, but that something had happened. Later, the police came, looked around, and took statements. There wasn't much I could tell them because I was in the town, and Michael wasn't here either. The neighbours were not that close to have seen anything. The house was a bit on its own. As soon as the police departed, I sat down and spoke with Michael. "Something dreadful has taken place, and we have to try and see if we can find out what it is. The police will be doing their bit. I think with her own dog which is a golden retriever, and with a good sniffer, we could get somewhere.

"If she's driven away," Michael said, "that would be very hard for the dog, wouldn't it?"

"Dogs are very clever. They can smell far better than we humans can. Some of them can pick up scent as far as a mile and even further. Heidi's dog will find her, I'm sure of that. We'll finish off what your mother was preparing, eat what we can, and then we'll be off hunting for her." I told Michael.

Bertram hadn't driven far, 50 meters down the dirt track from our house, then onto the tarmac road leading into a small wooded area where there was an old broken down water-mill. On his right side was a small bridge leading to a small wooden house; and at the side, to the back, a wooden water-wheel. The wheel wasn't turning any more, it had seen its day.

Bertram stopped the car just by the house, opened the back, and took Heidi out. He carried her to the house with its door half-broken down. Inside, he found the wooden stairs leading down to the cold, half lighted cellar. He took the gag off of her, and untied her hand, She said, "You horrible man, you won't get away with this. My man will get at you."

He said to her, "I'm a decent fellow. I'm doing this to teach you a lesson. I'm going to humiliate you for the way you talked to my sister. There are many women who found themselves in the same situation as my sister was in. But, you had to tell her off, making yourself more respectable than her, as if she was nothing. What do you expect your man to do anyway?"

"I expect him to deal with you like any man would do. He's not a coward. Wait and you'll see!"

"Take them off!" Bertram said.

"Take what off? What do you mean?"

"Take every bit of your clothing off. Do it right now!"

"I'm not doing it." Heidi told him.

Heidi had seen many films, and saw how some women were in the same situation as she herself was now in. She just had to play clever.

Michael was holding fast the lead of the golden retriever as it sniffed its way along the dirt track. We came to the tarmac road, and the retriever turned left, we followed it. Not far along, it turned up a small tarmac road, with us out of breath behind it. These dogs don't hold back once they pick up a scent. A few hundred meters up on the right, I saw the old water-mill. The bridge just in front of it slightly to the left. The wooden house was on top a stone foundation. At the bottom of this foundation was an archway where water gushed out. I told Michael to stay behind these thick bushes, and to keep the dog quiet while I go and have a closer look. There was a car at the right of the house. I did a complete recce of the place, and found that I get in through the archway where the water was coming from. Behind the house, a little distance away, water came from a source down a small makeshift hill, down along side the old broken down wheel. I went down in the water by the archway. It wasn't deep. Carefully I made my way in until I came to some stone steps leading up to a door. Soaking wet from my thighs downward, I peered through the glass frame. I could see lots of machinery, and just beyond to the right, I saw the big fellow, and standing there, was Heidi, completely naked. The blood rushed through me, and I grabbed the door handle and yanked it outwards.

He heard the noise and immediately came my way. We clashed on the drive-shaft that connected the wheel outside. Heidi started to make herself decent. I held on to the guy trying to jam his head between the two shafts, he was very strong, and I fail to do what I wanted to do. He slammed me into the board wall, and my whole body felt as if it had broken into a million of pieces. I was still in one piece and held on to the guy. We struggled for a bit on the floor, and then we both fell through the open door into the water. He fell awkwardly and I managed to get a grip on him, keeping his head under the water. I held on for a long time and noticed that his strength had gone.. I dragged him out of the water, up onto the grass, and then I gave him a hard right back hander across his face. Releasing myself from him, I stood up and saw the police looking down at us with their German Shepherd dogs. Michael was also there with the golden retriever. I walked up to Heidi and said, "You okay love?"

She gave a smile and assured me that she was okay. The police took the chap, put him in their van, and drove away.

Heidi, Michael, the dog and myself got back home safely. Michael didn't know of what took place in the cellar of the old broken down water-mill. We talked between us, then Michael went to bed. I said to Heidi,"You were very lucky today, for if it was another of those men who abuse women, it would have been worst for you. But thank God you're safe, and hadn't had to go through that."

"The man disgust me for doing that to me, humiliating me in that way."

"Some other criminal would have raped you, then kill you." I made it clear to her.

"I still don't like those type of people." Heidi said.

"There's quite a lot of them around."

"Let them keep to themselves, and not going around and molesting people." Heidi made her point.

"I think we need a few days holidays away from all this, don't you think so?" I asked her.

"Where shall we go? I think it's a good idea."

The following week, we left and went to a holiday park for a week. We took one that we know Michael would like and enjoy himself there.

7

The Ball Of Light

Coming back from the holiday park, something strange happened to us...

"LATE IN THE night we were on a long stretch of road - three lanes; coming back from holidays. Then we turned off and took a country road. Half an hour on, we found ourselves facing a strange light. There were different colours emitting from it, like the colours of the rainbow. I found too, that I had no control over the car. We drove straight into the light.

All we saw were images of ourselves, and we could not hold conversation with each other. This lasted for about ten minutes, and then we found ourselves back in the car, and driving along. "What was that?" Heidi asked. "It was like the mirror images that we see at the fair, but without the lights. It is the strangest experience I've ever had."

I said, "I've heard stories about such things, but to actually experience it, is something else. How did you feel Michael?"

Michael said, "It's the weirdest experience I've had as well. What was all that about? All those rainbow colours!"

"Was it more weird than you turn into an ant?" Heidi asked

"Turning into an ant and back again is not so weird as what happened to us not so long ago." Michael answered.

"What is strange is that there wasn't anything solid about it." I told Heidi and Michael.

Not very far from the ball of light the engine clonked out.

Everything went dead. Even the torches we had failed to work. There weren't traffic on the road. Now and then a car would pass We wondered if we were the only ones affected by the ball of light. Just then, two men came from the farm nearby, and asked if we needed help. They asked if we had seen the ball of light. We told them we went straight into it. They listened to our amazing story, looked at the car, got it running again, and we drove away from the area.

The following day at breakfast we all discussed what we had been through the night before. We came to the conclusion that we had definitely been through a weird experience. Michael knew nothing about UFO's and all the mysterious things of space. He was beginning to get interested in such things and we were willing to go along, and to tell him all that we knew.

"We can spend a lifetime here on earth, and still don't understand what's going on. There are so many theories." I said to Michael. "What happened to us is only a fraction, and still cannot be explained."

"I will get some books," Michael said, "and read up on the subject."

"That's a good idea," Heidi said. "But be warned, it's not an easy subject."

Michael said, "That's okay. I know, I'll manage somehow."

I said, If any strange marks appear on your body, let me know."

Michael asked, "Why should there be strange marks?"

"Well, you never know. Just in case, it's safe to check. I've heard stories where people found strange marks on them."

Michael went to the library and came back with a stack of books under his arms. "That's quite a lot of reading you got there." I said to him.

"I plan to read up on these mysterious things in space, especially the ball of light. The one we came through was completely empty, but there are some that encircle what they call a spaceship."

"Spaceships?" I said. "You're not going to tell me you believe in those things? We didn't teach you about anything of that stuff. It must have been from the TV that you picked up that information of them."

"There are lots of evidences in these books. They convince me that something is going on. Something strange." Michael said.

"You're still young," I said, "and you will find out later what a mysterious world we're living in. There's no solid evidence for these UFOs. The books are filled out with lots of reports and sightings, but no solid evidence."

"There was a group that took it upon themselves to investigate. And what they found is in one of the books I have here." Michael told me.

"Still, Michael, you can read about the mysteries, but keep an open mind. There are quite a lot that we do not know about. Space is a vast unknown area. We haven't so far made contact with any races or species, and I don't think we'll do for a long time to come yet." I said.

"But all these sightings cannot be nonsense!" Michael said.

Heidi came into the conversation after she had finished preparing food. "Nothing has been proven yet, Michael. One day something will happen."

"This space business sounds interesting. I'd like to see what I can learn."

"Oh! You'd learn quite a lot. But what to do with it, is the question." Heidi told him.

"According to the books I've got, people been seeing balls of light constantly. There's a report where two people were taken away in some strange light.

"And you believe that?" I asked.

"What about me turn in an ant?" Michael asked.

"We saw it, but we don't know what the experience is like, we've only heard it from you." I said.

"To be transferred to the community of an ant is something that I too cannot explain. It just happens. There has to be an explanation for all this. The ball of light, me, changing to an ant, all the reports I have here. Then you told me about space. Now I'm beginning to see that there's a power far greater than we. Is there another world that is spiritual?" Michael want to know.

Heidi said, "We know that we are physical, and the things we see around us. There has to be something spiritual or invisible, and that is the part we don't comprehend or cannot."

"There's something definitely spiritual or invisible," I said. "Take our brains, it record everything we do or see. And when we go to sleep, we're into a world of mystery. Our scientist says that there are many more solar systems out there, so you can see the possibility of having other species there, but that hasn't been proven."

The week came when Michael went away again with his father Edward. We hadn't heard anything more about Bertram or Melinda. Just outside the gate, the track led down to the tarmac road. On the left of the gate was a big farmer's field. From within our garden we can look out and see most of it. Around 8 pm, we saw a ball of light landed in the field. Heidi and I went to the gate to try and see what was going on. Out of the ball of light we saw these two creatures coming towards us. Before we had time to move away, they were already there beside us. They were tall, thin, and had faces like a snake. The next thing we knew, we were inside the ball of light. This turned out to be a shining silvery object like a cap turned over on another cap. It appears to us that the light inside were forever changing colours, like rainbow drops. We had never seen this before. The two creatures didn't have a mouth nor anything facial like us. They transmitted what they wanted to say to us, and we understood them. We saw too, this spiral contraption like a cork-screw going upwards and coming back down. The creatures told us that we'd be safe, no harm will come to us. On the right of us, there was this glassy ball with lots of coloured dots moving around. They represented the colours of the rainbow. We felt movement which was rather strange, and we couldn't recall anything more. There must have been some special reason why it was so important for us to be wearing those uniforms. Later, we found out that it was for the flight. The two creatures changed and we saw that they looked just like us humans. We followed them as they led the way to a door. Before we got to the door, it opened by itself. There was a sort of system there, looks something like ours, but much more simple. Into a sort of carriage car we went, covered over with what looked like glass. The speed was fast, fantastic. We got to our destination in no time. Then into a lift which took us to higher floors. I think we counted at least 12, as the lift went up. Then we were brought into a massive room. The commander came and greeted us. We were told many things that really surprised us. After the meeting, I was told that they wanted to take Heidi back to their home place on the 3rd solar system . I didn't agree with that, and so they let it rest. One of the two men who brought us up, gave me a small disc of the mother ship. We were taken back in the ball of light, and arrived just before Michael returned from his week's stay with his father Edward.

Inside the house, Heidi said, "Did that really happened to us or, were we dreaming?"

I said,"That was real. No one is going to believe us when we tell them about it. Not even Michael."

Heidi said, "What were you thinking then, when they said that they wanted to take me with them?"

"There was nothing I could have done, if they had done so. Maybe it's because of your blue eyes, and blonde hair, and also being tall, and beautiful." I replied.

"Do you think I'm beautiful?" Heidi asked.

"If you don't think so, I say yes, you are!"

"Thanks!" Heidi acknowledge.

"What did the commander said about the ship. I forgot." I asked.

Heidi told me, "He said it was 50,000 kilometres across."

"What?" I said, "you must have heard wrong."

"Those were the figures," Heidi said. "It's a massive ship, and we only got to see a little bit of it."

"Why did they take us to the mother ship?" I asked.

"Don't forget they could read us, and might know that we are 'okay people.'" Heidi told me.

"Okay people? You mean friendly people."

"Something like that!"

"I want to see the look on Michael's face when we tell him that we were on a ship circling the moon." I said.

"He'll think that we're having him on. We need to have something to prove to him that it is true." Heidi said.

"Well, would you believe it." I said. "One of the two creatures, I think I should say men, because they looked like us when they were on the mother-ship, gave me this." I showed her the small thing I had."

8

The Disc From The Mother-ship

On our way back from the Mother-ship, I was given a small souvenir.

HEIDI TOOK THE small disc from me and began to examine it. She found that it was very light, and that it had markings on it. There was a hole in the middle of it with small glossy things like crystal all round. It looked a bit like burnish bronze. She said to me, "What is this for? What can you do with it?"

I said to her, "He didn't tell me what it was for, he just gave it to me."

Heidi said, "It looks like some sort of device. Maybe they could keep contact with you through it."

"I don't think so," I told her. "It's probably a souvenir." Then suddenly, the disc came on with a voice, and where the hole was, there was a picture of who was speaking.

"See," Heidi said, "I told you it must be some device to make contact!" A picture was seen of one of them, the commander of the smaller space ship. "Greetings my friends!" The voice said. "Did you enjoy your experience with us. Hope you did. The object I gave you is to contact me any time. We are leaving your moon very soon. Sorry, I couldn't show you more of the mother-ship."

There were a few seconds before I spoke. I said, "Thanks very much. It was really a great experience for both of us. We cannot thank you enough. Have a good trip back."

The voice said, "Good luck! 3SG7," and the disc went dead.

"So we know now what the disc is for," Heidi said. "We're in communication with people from another solar system."

Edward and Michael came back. Michael looked great. He had a fantastic time. Edward stayed a while then he left. I urged Michael to tell us about his week away, which he did. After listening to what he had to say, I said to him, "Michael, we're going to tell you a story that is unbelievable."

Michael was waiting and listening. I looked at Heidi, then began to relate what had taken place while he was away.

"Mum and dad," Michael said, "I've heard many stories, but this one is way out."

Heidi said, "It did happen, Michael, just like your dad told you."

"It's hard to believe that my mum and dad been to space around the moon. There are many stories in the books I have, but my mum and dad? That's hard to take in.

"If I were you I would have felt the same way too," I told him.

Heidi said, "We can definitely prove to you, that our story is valid. Show him the device." I took the disc out and showed it to Michael. His eyes lit up when he saw it.

"Wow!" He said, "what is it for? Does it work? Is it a talking device? Say something in it!"

I got the disc in front of me, lowered my head, and said, "3SG7, 3SG7, 3SG7."

I waited, and then the commander of the small spaceship came on. Michael was amazed when all this happened. Now he knew our story was genuine, and not filled with fables. Finished speaking with the commander, the disc again went out.

"That was the commander who took us in the ball of light to the mother ship. They are very friendly people." I told Michael.

"You know what I found strange," Heidi told us. "Since we've been through that ball of light, nothing has happened to Michael to do with the ants!"

"Come to think of it," I said, "that's true."

"Michael said, "Yes, nothing has happened so far. But I wish I was here with both of you to experience that space trip. You told me that on your way up you couldn't recall how it all happened."

"That's true," I said. "We were our real selves again when we got to the mother ship."

"In the books I've got," Michael said, "there are some out of this world things happening. Cannot be explained."

"Your experience turn to an ant is one of them. And you yourself cannot really explain it to anyone without them looking at you funny." I said.

"There must be other species living out there in space." Michael told us.

"You know what was strange?" I told Michael. "The two men who took us to the moon orbit looked like snakes in their faces. It was a sort of outfit they were wearing."

Michael said, "So when they got back to the mother ship, they changed, and looked just like us humans.? That's amazing!"

I said, "Yes, it's amazing!"

"If they ever come back," Michael said, "I want to be there so that they can take me as well."

Heidi said, "We'll see what happens later on. Let's talk about your girlfriend."

Michael blushed, face red, then said, "She's a nice girl, lives a couple houses down from us. She's interested in the things I'm interested in, and is a couple years older than me."

I said, "That's good when you find someone whose interests are the same as yours. Things tend to go well."

"You mean like you and mum?"

"Well, yes," Heidi answered. "We sort things out properly."

Michael said, "Her name is Cathy, soon she'll be going away with her parents on holidays for four weeks. By the way, an invitation is given for us to come over when they get back."

Heidi said, "We have no engagements at that time, so it's okay. Does Cathy know anything about you change into an ant?"

"No," Michael answered. "I haven't mention the subject. It might scare her a bit If I happen to mention it."

I said, "I think it's best if you say nothing about it. But if she finds out, I wonder how she'll take it?"

Chatting a bit more, Michael left his mum and dad and went up to his room. He started thinking over how he must speak to Cathy, when she gets back, about his experiences. It wasn't going to be an easy task. If she was one of those who believe him, things would work out much easier. Michael knew he had a good education from home, he missed the community school but there was nothing to do about the situation. He was very good at playing the piano; brilliant with maths and English, and now he was getting very interested in science.

Cathy came back from holidays with her parents, and immediately visited Michael. They went out through the fields for a walk. She told Michael of all that had happened on her holidays which she had truly enjoyed. "How about you?" She asked Michael. "Did you go anywhere?"

"We stayed at home most the time, but we went visiting families. Mum and dad decided to take a rest this year because we had done much traveling earlier, seen many parks with their attractions."

"I like going to parks as well. One time we both must go together. I would like that!" Cathy said.

Michael took her by the hand, and they walked along briskly.

On their way back, Cathy saw a strange light that she had never seen before. She showed it to Michael, he knew what it was, and pretended it was new to him. He knew very well that he had a lot of explaining to do. This wasn't the time, so he said to her.

"People are always reporting seeing lights all the time, probably a reflection or something like that."

"But look," Cathy said, "it's coming closer and closer to us. Shall we run away?"

"Wait!" Michael said. "Let's not be afraid, and see what happens. Before Cathy could really make up her mind, the light landed not far from where they were. The two men with faces like snakes came close. Michael knew who they were, but Cathy didn't. She stood there shaking with fear. Michael told her that it was okay, they won't harm her. The two men knew who Michael was, and led Cathy and himself back to the ball of light, which was now a silver thing - shining brilliantly.

Cathy was in a dream world. She didn't think this was happening for real. They stepped into the ship, and her eyes almost popped with what she saw. She had never in her life seen anything like this before. How could she explain all this to her parents. They would think her mad. They wouldn't believe her.. The two men showed Michael and Cathy around, then they left again in a ball of light.

Nearing their homes, Cathy said to Michael, "They're really friendly, but I was scared to death at first."

Michael said, "Let's keep this to ourselves for a while, okay, Cathy? Don't mention any of this to your parents!"

"But I always..."

"I know, you always tell them everything, but could you please keep this our secret for now?"

"Okay! I'll do that." Cathy told Michael. "By the way, don't forget next week that your mum and dad are coming to my home, and of course, yourself as well."

"I know," Michael replied, then said goodbye to Cathy and went on home.

Michael came through the front door, and met his mum Heidi. She said to him, Ah! There you are! Everything okay?"

"Yes, mum. Those two men were here again," Michael told her.

"What two men? She had almost forgotten about those men who had taken her into space.

"Those men with faces like snakes."

"Did you meet them? Heidi asked.

"They took Cathy and myself and showed us around."

"How did she react?" Heidi inquired.

Michael said, "She was really frightened. Wanted to run away."

I came down from upstairs just in time to hear what had been said. "So Cathy knows about the ball of light?" I asked.

Michael said, "I'm afraid so, but I asked her not to tell her parents."

"That's a very hard thing you ask her to do," Heidi said. Some parents tell their children everything, and I'm sure that she'll tell them about that experience."

"She promised me that she'll keep quiet." Michael said. "We shall see their reaction when we go over to them."

Cathy's father was a well-built man, handsome and very peace loving. His job was a business man, and sometimes he was away from home for a few weeks. His wife, Cathy's mother, worked as a secretary in the town hall. She too, had a nice beautiful figure. She was just a little shorter than her husband. Heidi, Michael and myself met Cathy, her father and mother on the small porch. We all greeted each other. Michael knew them sometime now so he didn't need to introduce himself. Their house was beautiful. It was like a palace. It looked as if it just had been done over. Having seated ourselves down, and started chatting, the disc went off. Everyone was now looking at me. I took the disc out and heard the voice of the commander of the ball of light craft. I spoke with him for a few minutes. He told me about his trip and his meeting with Michael and Cathy. "In two weeks time," he warned me, "there would come a great storm over our area lasting for many days." I thanked him for the information and signed off. I looked at Harold and said, "Just friends from space."

"You mean the space station?" He asked.

I said, "No, very far away in space. They took us one time up to the moon where we entered the mother ship."

Heidi was looking at me in a way showing that she wasn't pleased that I was telling the story to Harold.

Harold said, "So we have some space people as neighbours, that's great?"

Mary said, "You all been to the moon? Michael didn't tell us anything about that."

Both Heidi and I were intellectual people, and I think Harold and Mary knew that. But they found what we said hard to swallow. It was while we were eating that Cathy said, "It's true. I saw the space people as well!"

"What is this Cathy, I hear from you? What sort of talk is this? Harold told her.

Mary was looking at her daughter, then to Michael. "Tell us what happened, " she said to Cathy.

Cathy stopped eating and said, "Michael and I were both out in the fields when we saw this light coming down over us. It landed, and two men with faces like snakes came over to

- 53 -

us. They took us to the craft which was silvery, and showed us around inside."

Harold said, "I have to believe you, Cathy, because I know you have never told us lies."

I said to Harold, "I'm glad that your own daughter has seen for herself that it was so, and that we weren't lying. The message I just got is about a storm that is due soon. I would make sure that everything around your place is safe. I will tell the local people about the storm."

"These people," Harold said, "seem very friendly and interesting!"

"They are," Cathy said. "Only that their faces are like snakes."

Heidi said, "They only look like that because of the kit they're wearing. On the mother ship, they look like normal human beings."

"Did they tell you where they came from?" Harold asked.

"Some where from the 7th solar system," I told him.

Harold said, "That is very far away. There are quite a lot of solar systems, and many stars with planets around them. We've been looking for some contact from those people for sometime now. What did you see on the mother ship?"

I answered, "There were many things that were shown to us. The mother ship is massive. We'll have the chance to see more of it if we're ever taken to it again."

We had a good evening with Harold, Mary and Cathy. Heidi said as we got back to our place, "Now they know about our contact with the space people."

"Harold doesn't think that it is silly because his own daughter told him she saw them. He was also up to date with the news."

I had already reported the storm to the local establishment. It came, did its damage and went away.

Michael had now many books on those alien people and

on the space projects. He began to tell us about black holes, and how they work. He told us that it was just space matter in one tiny place with a very strong gravitational pull. Even light cannot escape. We told him that we were glad that he has taken an interest into things that are really out of this world. Michael said, "With space being so vast, and we meet up with those aliens, there must be more out there on some of those other planets."

Heidi said, "Why do we go around thinking that we are the only one in the universe? It's like being on an island and thinking that there's no one else. For those who can comprehend, let them do so. This space business is a big mysterious thing."

On a July afternoon we were having a barbecue in our garden when we saw three lights coming down. Harold became excited, getting up from his seat, and moving over to the gate to have a closer look. They all came down in the farmer's field close to each other. In no time at all, they were all there at the gate, which Harold opened for them, and still in a sort of daze. Mary too, was looking a bit uneasy, and not herself, I told her it was okay, and to relax. This was something that she was never going to forget. There were six space people all with faces like snakes. But something caught my eye. The shape and slimness of one of them told me it had to be a woman. The commander whom we knew from our first meeting and his assistant came over and introduced the rest to us. I was looking at Mary to see how she was reacting to all this. But she was calm now. The commander told us that they had to take back some special plants with them. We all went over to the silvery crafts, and of course, they offered to take us to the mother ship for a day. Harold, Mary and Cathy couldn't believe it, especially to be taken to the moon, was awesome.

Inside the craft, we were given something to drink, just like we had the first time we went with them. At first, we heard a soft sound, and then a whining sound, and then nothing. We were in the mother ship that was in orbit around the moon quite some distance away. The space people whose faces looked like snakes were now normal looking people, and we of course, were our own selves again. We were deep down in one of the bays, and got ourselves up to where we wanted to be. The slim figure I saw back in my garden, was now the most beautiful creature I had ever set my eyes on. Blonde, blue eyes, tall, slim, she had it all. We got to see much more than we did last time. Harold, Mary and Cathy were taking it all in from up where we were we could see back on earth, oceans and continents. Later, we were taken in a circular vehicle from the mother ship and through an area of space.

It was like going through a tunnel, spiraling down and down. What a spectacular scenery of beautiful colors. We were looking at what could have been a master painting - all the colors mixed so beautifully. Then we came over a blue ocean with orange borders that looked like fire flaring up. This was really breath taking. Then the circular craft hovered there for a while as we enjoyed the view.

Back at the mother ship, the commander of the small space ship showed me a lot more what the disc can do. He did something so that we could see right back on earth, and our houses. I took all the information he gave me, then we went visiting places on the mother ship. As I said before, this mother ship was huge. We had to take a sort of transport that looked more like a pipe line. Examine it more, I saw that it had a sliding door that went back automatically. Then there was the capsule with seats. As we entered it, immediately it closed, and started moving at a fantastic speed. I learned later, that this system was without air. The capsule fitted precisely with its tube.

There was another system similar to that of our rail system, but here it was enclosed. Heidi and I had already traveled in that one. We talked with many groups of people, and learned a lot. Harold was amazed to see how friendly and sociable these space people were. In fact his family couldn't believe that they were actually experiencing this. But the commander had already told me that he knew that we were from his race. He told me about people who habited Mars, and went through terrible wars. Most of them, he said, had made their escape to other solar systems, and many went to earth.

The commander made it clear that he could not tell us everything because we weren't ready for that sort of stuff. In a room we saw an experiment of what supposed to be light, but could not see it. It was not visible to the eye. There are some things, he said, that are still mysterious in deep space.

9

The Custody Of Michael

We came back from around the moon only to find Michael's true parents asking for his custody.

THE SPACE SHIPS were ready down in the bay to take us back to earth. Everyone had enjoyed themselves, had seen things that no other on earth had ever seen. The mother ship itself was something to talk about - unbelievable.

We were there again in the farmer's field, back as normal human beings, knowing that we had just been to space around the moon. After saying goodbye to the space people, Harold, Mary and Cathy headed back to their place thanking us for that strange experience. We headed back to our own place. Heidi opened the door, and Michael and I followed in behind her. She took up the mail that was lying there on the floor. In the living room, she started looking through the mail.

"Look what I have here," she said. "Mail from the court of justice!"

I said, "Why would we be getting that sort of mail?"

Heidi had already opened it, and I could see in her face that it wasn't good news.. She sat down, read some more, and then passed it onto me. Having read the letter, I passed it to Michael. I said, "This is crazy business trying to claim Michael back from us. It was made clear in the beginning that we have all the right as parents."

Heidi said, "Now that Melinda, and Edward are both

claiming custody. Can we fight against them in court and win?"

Michael said, "I like my father, I had some good times staying with him, but I prefer to stay with you both. Why did they wait until I'm so old. I will blatantly refuse to go with them."

"I don't see how his mother could claim him when it was she who abandon him in the first place," Heidi said. "I have already told her what was on my mind."

"How do you feel, Michael, about your mother?" I asked.

"I can't really say because I don't know her. I haven't even met her"

"What can the higher court do, overrule what has already been stated?" I asked.

Heidi said, "They'll just listen to the case again, and because both parents are now claiming custody, it becomes a bit more complicated."

"My father has a good chance in getting custody of me," Michael told us. "He has a good job, is a nice and peaceful person. But as I have already said, my place is with both of you. I will tell the judge that too."

"I just remembered," I said, "the dog is still with your parents. Must go and get it tomorrow. Didn't you miss it?"

"Of course, I did. But with all that's been going on, it wasn't best to have it around."

"I still can't see how they could take away Michael from us," I told Heidi. "We'll have to get ourselves a good lawyer. We have the papers that we are legally the adoptive parents."

"Something must have really turned up to bring this about." Heidi said. "Maybe Edward had nothing to do with signing of papers. Then that could be why another hearing is called for. What is your grandfather like, Michael?'

"My grandpa is a nice man too, he wants me to come and stay with him. He spoke of that all the time."

"So then it is quite possible that he urged your father to take some action?" I said. "Your father has no problem with you being with us. He could see you whenever he wanted to."

Melinda has no chance whatsoever of getting Michael. Too many things are against her." Heidi said.

"Edward has a lot going for him." I told her. "We ourselves are in a solid position."

Gathered there waiting for the trial to begin, Melinda came over and hugged Michael, saying, "Oh, my darling, you have grown almost to be a man." Michael just stayed there being hugged by his natural mother, and didn't say or do anything. Edward and his father were there looking on, not very pleased of course, with Melinda. Cathy, her father and mother were there too. It was very plain to see that Michael didn't like his mother.

After the hugging, he was over and talking with his father and grandfather. Heidi and I were taking it all in, greeting the others who came along. An hour later, we all went in, and the trial started.

Our lawyer defended us well, he put up a good case. Melinda's lawyer had no chance whatsoever. Edward and his father had the same chance with us. Then Cathy was called to the witness stand.

Melinda's lawyer approached Cathy, he asked how long she knew Michael, Heidi and myself. She told him what she knew, making him understand that we were decent social people. "Isn't it true," the lawyer said, "that Michael once told you that he wants to get away from his adopted parents?"

Cathy looked the lawyer straight in his face, and said, "That is lie. He has never told me anything like that. Only about the space people."

"Space people?" The lawyer repeated. "What space people?"

– 60 –

At that moment, as Cathy blurted out "space people" I knew straight away, Michael would be taken away from us. Cathy told them the whole story, and it didn't go down well at all, even when they heard from Michael himself that those space people were friendly, but the judge, had other plans. Edward's lawyer weren't pleased at all when the subject of space people came to the fore. He couldn't understand why we were in contact with space people when the whole government had no shred of evidence that they exist. He found the whole thing strange, and it was in no way a good upbringing for Michael. We had done a good job so far, but he was thinking what sort of strange thinking Michael was into. Michael made it plain to them that what they heard about the space people was correct, and that he too had been reading about them.

The disc the commander of the small ship gave me, was not with me, it was back at the house. I was thinking that maybe I could have used it to prove my point, but it would not have made any difference. Then came the verdict that Michael is to go with his father and grandfather. Heidi was very sad when she heard it. Now it was a terrible blow. Michael also could not believe what he had heard. He had lived with us since he was a child, and now he found it hard that he should be leaving us. I saw tears come into his eyes, and a deep feeling came over me, you know, of parental love. It was all over. Michael was given to his father, and we went back home without him. The next day, his father came to collect his things.

There were no hard feelings between us; we were still able to see Michael whenever we wanted to. We took him out many times to the parks, just like we had done before. The space people were still in contact with us. We could have gone to the 7th Solar system with them if that was possible. For now, we just had to make our way forward without such a thing happening.

Months passed by, the house wasn't the same. With Michael around, it was different. Cathy visited often. She apologized for mentioning the space people. "You're a truthful person Cathy, and no harm done." I told her.

She and Michael were still seeing each other, that was good.

A couple months later, I got in contact with the commander of the small space craft, and told him all that had taken place. He said that they were at the moment in deep space, quite a long way from our Milky Way Galaxy. They had just examined a star 3 times the size of ours, and with 5 planets orbiting it. I asked him if there were anything unusual going on around the Milky Way. He said that it was heading on its course to meet Andromeda. They'd probably, he said, be in our area some time later again. He'll get more information about it.

Heidi and I did walk in the woods with the dog. And when we saw Michael again, we told him about the space people. He was thrilled to hear that. Then he said to me that I should have had the disc on me in court, where I could have proven that the space people were really friendly ones. I told him that our people weren't yet ready to accept the people from space. Even if the judge had seen and listened to the space people, he would have still given you to your rightful father.

Two weeks later, Heidi and I went with her parents to another town to look around. We arrived back late in our town in the afternoon. Coming out of the station to go and catch the bus, we saw a small crowd of people standing beside two cars that had a collision. Reaching over to where the cars were, a terrible shock came upon us when we got to the driver's side of the nearest car to us - it was Edward, slumped against the steering wheel dead, and in the back was Michael covered with blood. Next to Edward in the front, was his father, he too was dead. The ambulances came along with the police. Heidi was in a terrible state, but manage to get into the ambulance, along with myself to take Michael to the hospital.

In no time at all we were at the hospital. The ambulance pulled in under the archway, where there were already waiting, the duty nurses. Michael was taken in immediately into a room while we waited just outside. Time past very slowly before we were allowed to go in and see him. Laying there unconscious, I thought, my God, Michael, at least you're alive. Heidi and I both grabbed a chair, went and sat beside the bed, waiting to see some movement. Michael didn't come around that evening. He laid there not knowing that Heidi and I were there for him. We decided to stay around, to wait and see what would happen. It was early morning, the next day, when he opened his eyes and saw us. There were no real damage within , we were glad to hear that. He'd be able to walk and talk as normal, that was also positive. We phoned Cathy and her parents to let them know what had taken place. They too, visited often.

Michael spent a whole 2 weeks in the hospital, we going to see him daily and nightly. The time came for him to leave, and we took him home with us. We were the only ones who knew him well, and he would be safe and happy with us. Finally, the court order for keeping Michael was changed back to us again. We were now without any more upset, the adoptive parents of Michael.

The days that followed saw us making sure that he was completely well, and himself again. It was not possible for him to attend his father's and grandfather's funeral, for he was in no fit state to do so. It hurt him very much, and the memory of them would stay with him. After getting his belongings, he was back in his old home. Things were back as they were before. Lots of discussions on space and the space people, the power of human beings on earth, and where they were heading for.

A message on the disc told that the space people would be in our area next year around May. They had found another system with five suns, and only one planet orbiting them; there'll be no night there. They had also found a part where space didn't move, it was fixed.

Heidi, Michael and I were looking inside the disc, and were amazed at the things we saw. Black space with no stars or any light. A milky way with beams of light through it. Michael said, "How could life like us be living out there on some planet. They have to be living on some space ship like our space people."

I said, "Our space people have their home on the 7th solar system. There could be other species with the ability to live there."

Heidi said, "It is really fantastic to see the beauty of it all. So many strange things happening as well."

Michael said, "I really like those space people, can't wait to see them again."

10

The Marriage Of Michael And Cathy

*It didn't come as a shock to anyone when the news came out
that Michael wants to marry Cathy.*

IT HAD BEEN going pretty well between Michael and Cathy.
Their relationship was really good. Then Heidi and I learned
that Michael wants to Marry Cathy. Her parents agreed, and
we had no objections at all. We thought, they'd make a good
couple. Both interested in the same things in life.

Everything was settled. The day came when the event was
to take place. There was something unusual about the guest
list: it had 'space people'. They didn't come to the Town Hall
where the wedding took place, but at the reception. Later that
day. We had told them on the disc, what was taking place,
and the commander of the small space craft, along with his
co-pilot showed up. They didn't stay long, and left certain
people amazed and asking all sort of questions. The wedding
went down well, there were many people gathered there and
watching, making comments, for Cathy was wearing this
beautiful white embroidered dress, with not too long train. She
looked the part of a princess. Michael wore long grey trousers
with a well-cut blue jacket hanging long at the back, and short
at the front. He too, looked like a prince.

After the ceremony was over at the Town Hall, all the
invited guests found themselves at the reception which was
about 200 metres away. There was an official photographer

taking pictures. Heidi and I were also taking some pictures on our mobiles.

At the reception, the guests were all there as Michael and Cathy arrived. They were given drinks and then introduced to all the guests, even those who were not able to be at the Town Hall. After the meal is served, many toasts were said. Emails were read by the best man, who officiated, and knew Michael from his old school, and still a best friend. We had a good laugh listening to some of the emails that were read. Michael and Cathy went over, and together they cut the cake, and went back, sat down, and tasted it. Off they went up on the dance floor while everyone watched. Heidi and I joined them, along with Harold and Mary. The whole dance floor later, was packed. We had some afters, and then we gathered as Cathy threw her bouquet of flowers in the crowd. They said their last goodbye to all, and was off to their honeymoon destination.

Driving along the road to their honeymoon hotel, Michael and Cathy were seeing strange lights, they knew why that was so. It was the space people. After two hours Michael and Cathy came to their hotel.

The hotel was a few kilometres from the main road. Beautifully situated next to a small sandy beach, and had its own swimming pool. Michael and Cathy could now relax and enjoy their honeymoon.

Heidi and I helped Harold and Mary in preparing the flat for when Michael and Cathy came back. They had given instructions before the wedding, how they wanted it decorated.

Arriving back from their honeymoon, Michael and Cathy were very pleased in the way the flat was done up. They told us that they had a fabulous time. We all sat around and looking at all the pictures including the wedding ones.

One day while in Cathy's parent's garden, I saw a worried look on Michael's face. I went over to him and said, "Let's go for a walk."

While we were walking, I asked him if something was troubling him. He said, "everything's OK, only that I'm thinking, should I tell Cathy about my experiences turning to an ant and back? How would she take it? She has experienced with all of us, the space people. But for her to understand what it feels like to be an ant, is something far different."

I patted him on the shoulder, then said, "I see what you mean, I would have had the same problems, not knowing what to do. Cathy is a true girl, she doesn't hide anything from you or her parents. I still think that you should keep the ant experience that you had, to yourself. It is true that she could hear of it from those who know you back when you was in school. But so far, she hasn't heard anything. How would she act when you should tell her about it? It is really something hard to take in. Since we met up with those space people, your contact with the ants came to an end. Have a chat with Heidi and see what she says."

Michael said, "If I don't tell her, it would be as if I am cheating on her, not telling her about it."

"I am thinking," I told him, "if she accepts the space people, then she might believe you when you tell her about your experience with the ants. It's quite possible, she might laugh her head off about it."

Michael spoke with Heidi. He always get good answers from her. She told him not to tell Cathy now, but to wait until sometime later. Whatever you do, she told him, he must not lie to her.

Inside their flat, after some months had passed, Cathy went to Michael and whispered something in his ears. His eyes lit up, he slung his arms around her, and held her tightly. "That's great news, Cathy," he said. "You'll make a great mother. I love you."

She kissed him and said, "I love you too."

A baby girl was born to Michael and Cathy, and both families celebrated. They named the baby Bernice. At this time, Michael started seriously writing about space, and the space people whom we knew. Michael was thinking now, that it was a good time to break the news of his experience with the ants, to Cathy.

Cathy had the baby in its cot in the bedroom while she was in the kitchen preparing a snack. Michael was visiting her parents. As she turned and came out from the kitchen, she saw this line of ants. It baffled her for a few seconds, because she didn't know where they came from. The flat had always been kept up to a high standard in cleanliness. She placed her snack down, and followed the trail of the ants that led her back into her own bedroom. When she got to where the cot was, she got a shock, one which frightened her. There was only an ants nest in the cot, and no baby.

Cathy was definitely frightened, but not a fright to drive her mad. She was a strong and steady woman. Looking around everywhere, she still did not see the baby. Using her mobile, she phoned Michael and told him what happened. Michael got onto me and told me what had taken place. Heidi with the dog and myself went over to the flat. Michael was already there with Cathy's parents.

Seeing the ants was nothing new to Michael, Heidi and myself, and to think about it, the dog as well. Harold and Mary had never seen the like, and found it rather mysterious. Michael took Cathy aside and was about to tell her why the ants were there, hesitated, and didn't do so. Then I remembered the disc,

I had it on me. Without Harold and Mary seeing what was doing, I went and placed the disc inside the cot. Immediately, the baby was there, and the line of ants disappeared. I replaced the disc back into my jacket pocket. Cathy and her parents knew that I had the disc, and wasn't surprised when I used it. Cathy took the baby from the cot, in her arms and went to the living room where we all sat down and chatted.

Harold said to Mary, "I think we have an extraordinary grandchild. We'll have to be careful when we take her out walking, when she grows up, that she doesn't disappear on us!"

"Mum and dad," Cathy turned to her parents, "that's not going to happen. Bernice will turn into a fine young woman."

Bernice was a year old when Michael told Cathy that he had something to tell her. Cathy, in the living room was waiting quietly to hear what Michael had to say. He said, "I've been wanting to tell you this for a long time, but I didn't know how to tell you. With all that was happening, I decided to wait."

"Is it something bad? Has it got to do with another woman?"

"No, nothing like that!" Michael said. "Before I met you, I used to turn into an ant."

"Am I hearing right?" Cathy asked. "An ant? Then that would explain why the ants were in our flat. I know there are certain mysteries in our world, and I have experienced being with the space people, but turning into an ant, that has taken first prize."

"What are you going to do, now that you know the truth?"

Cathy said, "I have to think about it, give me some time!"

"You're not going to leave me?"

"Why should I do that?" Cathy asked. You will still be my husband, as long as you don't go turning yourself into a rock. Turn yourself into an ant for me now!"

"I can't," Michael said. "It used to happen before, but since I had the experience with the space people, it stopped."

"Really, Michael? Your loving wife wants to see this miracle of yours."

"I'll let my mum and dad explain that to you, then maybe you'll believe what I'm telling you."

Cathy went and got her suitcase.

"What are you doing?" Michael asked her.

"Can't you see," she said, "I'm packing to leave."

"But you can't do that! We only just got married!"

"Seeing that you won't turn yourself into an ant for me, I will leave."

"Please stay, Cathy. You know that we love each other."

"I know that," she said. "I'm only having you on. I'm not going to leave you."

Michael was relieved when she said that. He thought that she was seriously going to leave him.

Cathy said, "I believe what you have told me, and I have seen what has happened not so long ago. I put two and two together, then realize the truth of the matter. Your daughter has inherited it from you."

Michael said, "It doesn't happen to me any more since I came into contact with the space people, and I hope it will be the same for Bernice after what has happened."

Cathy said, "You and I, Michael, will never ever part. We'll stay together forever."

"I feel the same way too," Michael told her.

Michael had to tell Cathy all about his experience as an ant, and how they lived. She found it very interesting.

11

War Between Earth and Space People

Things got out of hand when a group on earth located one of the small space ships.

THERE WAS A group interested in strange objects in the sky, and at this time, were keeping watch around where the space people always landed. The space people had this system of making their spaceship, which was a small one, not to be visible. If you were in the area, you wouldn't know that there was a spaceship there. The earth group had some modern technical instruments such that can detect invisible things. They had heard many reports about the area, and decide to check it out. With their infra-red equipment, they cordoned off the area. Inside a van, they had a radar using micro-wave beams. The space people came down in their craft and was trapped.

They couldn't lift off, everything went dead. The mothership knew what was going on, and had already sent 6 smaller ships down. It took them no time at all. They hovered over the area where the small craft was damaged. The commander and his pilot were taken aboard on one of the six crafts. Using a device, they got rid of the craft without leaving any trace of it. Then they return to the mothership.

On the disc I had, we were told what had happened, that our people had become dangerous, and it was impossible to come to our area. I told them about the birth of Bernice, and they were pleased with the news.

The commander of the small craft warned me that his people are not at all happy with some of the people on earth, and that they were planning to teach them a lesson. He said we were safe where we were for they knew the location very well. We the space people are very advanced and peaceful, but we shall show the earth people a thing or two. Whenever we land, they have the means to locate us, but in space, we change to light at tremendous speed. I cannot tell you much more, soon, it will happen. Warn your officials so that they know. I said to him that my officials would laugh at me, when I tell them what you told me. You still have to tell them, he said to me. The disc went off, and I turned to Heidi. "Our space people are going to attack the earth!"

"How could they do that?" Heidi asked. "I thought they were people who didn't like war?"

"They are peaceful, Heidi, but they have to protect themselves. Having had one of their spaceships attacked by an amateur group, they're now going to retaliate, and teach earth a lesson."

"Why couldn't they forgive?"

"Space people are not like us. There are many groups out there in space each with its own sophisticated system. We are lagging behind."

"Our earth people are foolish," Heidi told me. "Why couldn't they accept the space people, and exchange information? Those space people would not have been here if they were not looking for something, that something has to be important as well."

"It;s too late now," I said. "They have declared war on earth people."

"How can earth defend themselves from such mysterious space weapons?" Heidi shook her head. "This is absolutely foolish!"

"Maybe it is, but it's going to happen."

"Shall all the nations join together against the space people?" I never ever dreamt of such a thing happening." Heidi told me.

"When the attack starts, countries are going to blame each other. Not knowing that it came from space. For if the space people attack the North, the North would think it came from the West. And it could be the same, if the West came under attack, they would think it came from the North. That's why I have to tell the officials, and let them sort that one out."

A few days later, the whole earth was plunged into darkness. The space ships had moved away from the moon, and was now orbiting Saturn. After the week's darkness was over, there came an enormous quantity of meteorites down upon the earth, followed by a number of hairy comets. They did no damage, but came close enough.

The nations all knew now what they had to do. A meeting was held, and together, they came up with a plan, to try and defeat the space people. The mother ship of the space people was an enormous thing, but it was protected from incoming missiles. It also had quite a number of small spaceships that could change themselves into light, and back again.

These ships would be used to damage earth's nuke installations. They had no intention of destroying their space rockets. Space people had so many of these small ships, that they could cover the complete space around the earth. This was rather dangerous for earth people. Earth people were stubborn, they didn't give up. With their plan, as soon as the ships changed from matter into the next, they had special missiles to fire at them.

Earth people found it hard to hit one of the space people ship because they were protected with an invisible shield. Much damage had been done to the North, some Eastern places as well. Quite a number of nuclear plants had been wiped out. A meeting was arranged between the top space people, and top officials on earth. It was decided that the space people would take control of earth for five years, then hand it back to earth after they were satisfied with how things were going.

Bernice was now five years old when the earth was given back, no longer under the command of the space people. We were all in my garden, Michael, Cathy and Bernice. Harold and Mary. Heidi, myself and the dog. Two of the space people turned up and they took Bernice to their craft, and brought her back. This was her first experience of the space people. I said to Bernice, when the space people had left us, "They're our people, who live high up in the sky. They look after us, visiting us now and then. Were you afraid when you saw their faces?"

She said, "Yes, grandpa!"

"They're not always like that. Only when they're visiting. One day you'll see them how they really are."

Harold said, "I'm glad this war is over. What were our people thinking of, trying to take on the space people?"

"That's typical earth," I said. "Ready to take on anything, but they met their match with the space people."

Mary said, "I'm glad they made peace. The space people doesn't want war."

Heidi said, "We're just only learning new things about space. There's still a long way to go."

Michael was listening to everything that had been said. "I hope you all will read my book when it comes out!"

"How far are you with it?" I asked him.

"I'm at the moment explaining black holes, and the enormous gravity they have; and how light can be sent to another area in space. Nothing comes back out of that hole." Michael said. "I have to get more information about the solar systems, and the many suns with planets around them. But there's one thing: they have not yet seen a planet the same as earth. They have seen planets that are near enough like earth, but not exactly like earth."

Cathy said, "I've read some of the manuscript, and it's pretty good."

Looking back over the years, I was very pleased now the way things turned out. It was my lucky day when I first met Heidi, that was a real treat. One couldn't ask for anything more. Together we had battled through life, taking the good with the bad. Our adopted son, Michael, had done really well for himself. I was also thinking of the space people. They are a friendly race. At the end of the day, when all had gone, and only Heidi, the dog and myself left, I said to her, "Are you happy?"

She said, "Yes, I am! And you?"

"Oh! I'm more than happy. Life is so wonderful even with the negative things around."

"That's what it was made for, to enjoy every minute of it, and not to murmuring all the time."

"Some people are really good at that!" Heidi said.

12

Bernice's Holiday Trip

We decided it was time to take Bernice to one of the holiday parks.

WE GOT NEWS from the space people that they're leaving Saturn. It was getting too windy there, and the small crafts couldn't land physically on it. They're planning to go to Neptune, and try and see what they make of Triton

A trip had already been planned. Bernice would see one of the parks her father visited when he was young. It was about 62 kilometres away. We were ready when the day arrived. Harold and Mary stayed home. We took the dog with us. Ten kilometres into the journey, the road stretched out, going down, then up, and then a long level stretch. On either side, were thick woods. The car we hired was a long green estate, very comfortable, it had plenty of room. On a level stretch, we saw this police car with flashing lights on top. I slowed down, and along came this policeman. I said to Heidi, "I don't like this at all."

Michael and Cathy were in the middle seat with Bernice. The dog and our luggage were in the back. Another policeman came up but I couldn't see his face properly.

They told us that they had to check people coming through this area, and needed to see some identification from us, Both had shown their police badges. The car engine was running, and I had the window down. The dog was uneasy and began to bark. Then I knew something was really wrong.

The first policeman took the papers while the other was looking inside the car. I saw the figure of a woman in the back of the police car. As soon as he gave me back the papers, with the car already in gear, I slammed my foot down on the gas peddle, and the car shot away, like a bullet, leaving the two policemen amazed, but running to get their car.

In my car everyone was OK. There were a few more kilometres to go before we came out this wooded area, and to the next village. Luckily, I wasn't driving too fast when the left rear tyre blew.

I controlled the car and pulled in off the road, looking to see if the police car was any where in sight. Everyone was still OK, with no smile upon their faces. Getting out and going to the back, the other came close by. The two men got out of the car, came up and said, "That's as far as you go." Then he shouted for everyone to get out the car. The dog was going wild, but was kept on the lead. Evening was falling, it was getting dark, but I still had time to see the face of the second man, it was Bertram, and in the car was Melinda.

She came out the car, walked up to Heidi and slapped her across the face, Heidi slapped her back, and said, "How dare you, you horrible woman?"

"You're in my power now," Melinda told her, "and you'll have to beg for mercy."

Michael was angry, he placed himself between Heidi and Melinda. Bertram and the other man who was his accomplice ordered us on a track in the woods, off the road. I know now I had to play this game the way its supposed to be played. I didn't want anyone to get hurt. I said, "Cant we be decent people and talk this whole thing out?"

Melinda said, "Talk what out? You've cut me off from my family, no invitation to my son's wedding, and not even let me see my grandchild. She reached out and took hold of Bernice who was now very much disturbed from all that had taken place. Michael was holding on to the lead of the dog that was really barking its head off. He tried to calm it down, but that was not possible. Melinda told her brother and the other man to get hold on me, and they know what they should do. Just then, a car pulled up beside our broken car, and shouted up to us if we needed help. "Yes, we do." I shouted back. The people in the car got out - four of them - and started seeing what they could do. They were army soldiers going back to their base. They were big fellows, and I saw how Bertram and his friend behave. There was nothing they could do now seeing that we had company. All three of them went to the police car, and drove away.

The soldiers helped me with the spare, and I thanked them, and we were on our way again. Heidi said, "If that car hadn't come along at that moment, God knows what would have happened!"

"That Melinda is just out for revenge even when there are kids around!"

Michael said, "We should have let the dog sort them out!"

I said, "We acted in a good way. I'm glad it went off the way it did."

Cathy said, "My mum and dad won't believe when I tell them the story."

Heidi said, "That was your mother , Michael. She showed you what she's like."

Traveling the rest of the way, everything went well. We got to the holiday park, and found our chalets. It was a beautiful sunny day when we woke up next morning. Bernice was ready to enjoy herself. After breakfast, we all went out and started looking at the different attractions, the lit-up stalls, the many turning wheels, the pony rides, and many more. For the four weeks we stayed at the holiday park, Bernice enjoyed herself, and we took many photos that she could later look back on. At the end of it all, we drove back home.

13

From Earth To Fifth Solar System

The space people were right with the information about the earth.

The space people found a solar system with a planet where earth people can survive. They told us that they wanted us to come and live there because it would be peaceful and also safe. Earth, they said, would soon be in much trouble.

Michael thought that it was a great adventure going into deep space to live. Of course, the space people would be transporting us there. But what about leaving our home on earth? That would be a real risk to take. We've known the space people for quite sometime now, and everything they had told us was good. Heidi didn't really like the idea, but said that if it had to be so, then there was nothing we could do about it. She much prefer to stay on earth.

Harold and Mary when they heard about it said that it was not for them. They don't mind going and have a look, but to stay there was not appealing. Michael and Cathy was all for it. It would be like going to another country that they'd never been to before. And with Michael deeply interested with space, it would be a big hit for him. Bernice was still a bit too young to understand what was going on Earth people had gotten lots of secret information from the space people on how to build small space crafts, and mother ships. The ships should be build in inner space. The mother ships can be of any size, but it would also be wise to give them a slow spin.

"I'm not worrying too much," Heidi said, "because our sun has billions of years left, and the earth will still be in one piece, I won't even be around."

"I think what the space people are trying to do is to prepare us for that day that they know will come about." I said.

Michael said, "I could see it actually happening. Earth transporting people to a far away solar system, but not everyone will be taken there."

"I've got this theory, Michael," I said. "Saying goodbye, the sun will hand over to the earth which will then be a ball of fire burning in space, taking the place of the sun."

"So you mean, it will be light for the solar system? Not a bad theory, but I can't see it happening."

Heidi said, "We need to be living our lives, and not to be thinking too much about these distant things. Oh, but you Michael, I forgot that you are busy thinking of these things."

Earth was now preparing for a big evacuation. Mother ships were now high up in space, and waiting for the smaller ships to bring the people there. The scientists knew that our moon had been slowly moving away from the earth - no longer in the gravitational pull - and would no longer be turning around the earth. The only thing that they reckoned could happen is that it would plunge into the earth, making the whole earth a watery mass.

Within this year, they said, it could take place. Unfortunately, not everyone would be able to be transported away. I said, "At least, we have our space people to take care of us, and now Harold and Mary have to come along."

Heidi said, "I was thinking that such a thing like that would be a long way off yet. Now here we are having to leave everything behind."

"You can start a new life on the new planet, and forget about earth because it cannot inhabit any life." I told her.

"It's not going to be easy to forget about earth in a hurry." Heidi said. "I'm taking this album with me, to look back on some of the photos."

"It's not possible for you to take the album, you can record it on the disc. Up in space, you can settle on the new home, and things will carry on as normal," i said.

"Are there any creepy, weird things up there?" She asked.

"I don't think so," I said. "This is a clean planet with no animals on it."

"No pets?" Heidi said, "that's going to be a bit boring for us. Later, they'll probably transport animals there. I hope they're not horrible!"

"It's a planet where there are many crystals. Houses there are made of them. And there's the 'Blue Ocean', clear like crystal." I told her. "We'll not be in the same light as that of earth, we'll be totally changed."

"Does it rain and gush down like it does here on earth?" Heidi asked.

"There's no rain on that planet!"

"How does plants and all that survive?" She was amazed.

"The system there is rather different, there's a lot of electromagnetic light waves in operation there." I told her.

"Sounds extraordinary!"

"Yes, it is!"

"What's the name of the planet?" She asked.

"Nepsi," I said, "and you can see it on the disc."

I got the disc and tuned into Nepsi, the planet came into view. The skies over the planet were multicoloured, beautiful like in a dream.

"What I don't understand," Heidi said, looking in the disc at the 'Blue Ocean', "is, how can you have water, and no rain falls upon the planet?"

"The 'Blue Ocean," I told her, "looks like water, but it is not water as we know it."

"I want to see all this when I get there!"

News came that there was a comet heading for earth. Evacuation started before the planned date. Many people found themselves in space inside the mother-ships. Our space people came and took us away. We were transported to Nepsi. Heidi couldn't bring her dog with her, so she left it with her parents. I felt pity for all those who were left behind. I wished they all could have come with us, but that wasn't possible.

Earthquakes erupted all over the planet with tsunami here and there. Volcanoes blasted up in the skies with fire and billowing smoke. Poor earth, to go through such terrible disasters! In earlier days, earth had a taste of all those disasters, but human beings had not yet been formed. It is amazing how beautiful space is.

Moving away from our solar system, we moved into interspace, and seeing galaxies of all sorts. Black holes whirling around, light emitting from everywhere. Dark-red stars on their last legs, not expanding any more. We could see the bar of light and its four entrances, all filled with stars. So many stars to look upon. Moving on, and arriving at the 5th solar system. There we saw Nepsi orbiting its star, and also the red dying star. Nepsi has to make a journey of 700 days around its own sun; and 7 years around the dying star, still in its gravitational grip. The colours around red star are really breath-taking.

Hovering there, and looking at the sight for sometime, then we descended and landed safely on Nepsi.

Heidi said, "So this is Nepsi, it's beautiful, and all those crystal houses!"

"Wait till you see the 'Blue Ocean', your eyes will pop out!" I turned to Bernice who was with her parents, "When you get older, you have a lot to tell"'She shook her head.

Harold and Mary couldn't believe what they were seeing. They had seen other parts of space, but here on Nepsi, it was too much. The houses so beautiful with the different colours of light sparkling from the crystals. The space vehicle was out of this world. They'd never seen any transport like this before, or will ever see again. A change had come over all of us. We felt as if we were different people. Still in the human form, we didn't do the things that we did when we were on earth. There's no craving for food, or wanting to go to the WC every minute, and the thought of sex didn't enter into our minds. The day was very hot, hotter than one of earth's hot summer days. They brought us to our quarters, all made from crystals, clear as ever. People outside can see you inside. The commander of the small space ship had a chat with us, told us that we'll be safe here, and that at nights it gets rather cold, when we are outside. After chatting with us, he returned to the mother-ship.

More and more crafts were coming down with people from the earth. There was something that had been bothering me for sometime. The opportunity had come for me to get it off my chest. Just before the commander of the small craft went back to the mother-ship, I had the question for him. "How do your people have children?"

He told me that both the male and female would go into a room where they were connected to a machine. Then both of them would start thinking of a child. And there on the screen the form would take place. If the man has too much positive, it becomes a girl, and if the woman too much positive, it becomes a boy. A child is then born already grown to the age of 9. I think he already knew how we on earth have our babies. I wonder what he was thinking about that, or not thinking about it at all.

Our houses on Nepsi were beautiful. There was the bedroom, big and long. Above our heads were clear crystal. There were two other bedrooms, no kitchen, no WC. On both side of the bedroom, there were long crystal doors. On the opposite side of the bed was a crystal case with a disc just like the one I have.

Harold and Mary's house were exactly the same. So was Michael and Cathy. They were all pleased. The commander, before he left, had told us about the space vehicles, and showed us how they worked. They can take you anywhere on Nepsi. Nepsi was just a little bigger than earth. Our main aim now was to go and see the 'Blue Ocean."

We'd be there in no time in the space vehicle. We were also told that the lights in the buildings at night, came on automatically. There were now many people on earth living on Nepsi. Earth had been damaged badly, but not all of it. We tuned in with the disc and saw all the damage that was done to the earth. The area where Heidi's parents lived was okay. It hadn't been hit. "Do you think that they are still alive?" She asked me, looking on eagerly.

I said, "I'm sure they're okay!"'

There we were, all like kids looking at the 'Blue Ocean.' It looked like it had layers and layers of what looked like water. It gives one the impression that if you touch it, it would collapse into itself. It was something I had never seen before or never dreamed of. There were circles all around like a big wave curled in onto itself, and then spread out. The beauty of the whole thing was just fantastic. After enjoying seeing the 'Blue Ocean', we went around looking at other places, then everyone of us went to their own quarters.

The living room was circular and laid out magnificently. Next to that was the rest room. I said to Heidi, "It was worth it to come here, wasn't it? I mean, apart from the damages done to earth, we couldn't do anything about that."

"It is really something, that's true. You hear people talking about heaven or paradise - this is it - in all its glory! "

"This is the 5th Solar System," I said, "but there are many more that people like us would not get to see!"

"But why so many?" Heidi asked.

"Just the way it all is," I told her. "It has baffled many a scientist, left scratching their head, perplexed. Generations will come and generations will go, and still there'll be secrets left untold."

"Back on the mother-ship, I didn't see anyone getting hurt, and being treated. Maybe, we are now the same. This body cannot be damaged!"

"Look here," I said to her, pointing to the disc. "There's your parents!"

Heidi looked in and saw her parents both in the living room watching TV, with the dog beside them. She was excited. She shouted, "Hi mum and dad!" They could not hear her.

Without a disc like ours, it was impossible to hold contact with them. This disc we have been good, because we could tune in anywhere in the universe.

"Back home," I said to her, "we would be busy cooking up something and watching TV together. Talking about TV, I wonder what's on for entertainment on this disc. I tune in to see what I could find, but only programmes about space came on. Programmes that we should be picking up from the earth are blocked on this disc. Heidi said to me, "There are many people on Nepsi, and many were kept back behind because of the confusion and eruptions that were going on. We saw on the disc how badly earth had been damage, and it's absolutely amazing that my parents escaped it all!"

"They were in an area that was not affected." I told her.

Our days on Nepsi went down well, all the people who were brought up from earth were now in one area. We saw quite a lot of Nepsi, and traveled often.

In the summer of Bernice's 8th year, some people came from the 3rd Solar System in strange banana-like space crafts, and took over the planet. They weren't as friendly as our space people. Our space people had seen what was taking place and had sent some small fighting space ships from their home on the 7th Solar System. I was on the disc to the commander when two of the men from the 3rd Solar System came to us. They wanted to know where we were from because Nepsi had no one on it for a long time. We told them where we were from, and learned that they didn't like the earth people.

They took away the disc from me, and took Heidi and myself up to the mother-ship. Their mother-ship was shaped like a big round table at both ends with a long barrel shaped joining them. All around the mother-ship, were small ships, patrolling, quite some distance away.

At one end of the ship, which was table shaped, there were on the outside rim, a sort of travel system, like a bowl shape thing that we sometimes see at the circus. You go in it, and it start spinning around. This one on the mother-ship had seats in it, and would take you around any part of that area. Heidi and I were held in a beautifully decorated room. And the view out of it was spectacular. Then some people came in, about three of them. They carried on asking more questions. I noticed that there was a flat panel just outside the door, and when they came to it, the door had opened.

It didn't take our space people long to arrive on the scene. It was very hard at first to see what was taking place because the space ships of our people had the ability to change themselves into light and back again. Those from the third system, were not capable of doing so. They were quickly defeated. The mother-ship of the 3rd Solar System people was taken over, and Heidi and I were taken back to Nepsi. I was given another disc. The one Heidi had her photos on could not be recovered. The enemy on Nepsi were overpowered, and things were back as they were. We told the rest about what happened to us up on the enemies mother-ship.

The space people were busy looking around to see if they could find more solar systems with earth-like planets. So far, they hadn't found anymore. They found double-stars, and triple-stars. They knew that there were other groups around on some other solar systems, but hadn't made contact with any of them, only the ones from the 3rd Solar System whom they had the battle with.

14

Return To Earth

The space people knew about the red star that Nepsi had to go around, but they didn't know that it would cause so many problems.

THE RED STAR that Nepsi had to go around was now behaving badly. Now and then, it would flare up causing the inhabitants on Nepsi to wonder what was going on. Would it calm itself down and flare up no more? No one knew exactly what to say about the red star. Even the space people hadn't a clue how it would behave in its final stages.

Some red stars just finally die out, while others had flared up so enormously, that they took in the planet that orbit them. This was terrible news. At anytime then, the red star could flare up, and we on Nepsi could be no more.

Nepsi was not completely populated. The people that were brought up from the earth were situated in one area. There were no mountains on Nepsi, it was flat as a pancake. The people from the 3rd Solar System had left one of their ships in an area about 5 kilometers away from where we were. Heidi and I decided to go and check it out. I was very good with electrical and mechanical things, but a space ship was something different - more advanced, more sophisticated. Traveling in our vehicle, we were there in no time. This ship of theirs was something, it was a treat just to be looking at it. The metallic silver-like rim shining smoothly covering what looked like another thin rim, followed by another looking at it from a distance, it looked like three wheels, with just a gap between them. Heidi said, "Wow! We saw them when they first arrived, but not close up like this. How are we going to get inside?"

Heidi wasn't just a pretty face with lovely blue eyes, she was extremely clever. I said to her. "You have asked the greatest question of the year! I haven't the slightest idea how we are going to do that!"

The ship was big enough to take a few people on board. We looked it over some more, trying hard to find where the entrance would be. We just could not pick up a place where there could be an entrance. Heidi said, "What about the disc? Could that help?"

"You've won yourself first prize," I said to her jokingly. "Why didn't I think of that?"

With the disc held in my hand, I moved it across the area where a door should be; if there was one. We heard movement, panels started sliding left and right. There were about three different sliding panels. Then we were confronted with a door with a small crystal square, just on the right. "Now what?" I asked. Do we need some code to get in?"

"Try passing your hand over it," Heidi told me. I did that but nothing happened. I looked to the disc for more instructions. Those men from the 3rd Solar System had taken us back to their mother-ship, and I remembered seeing this same crystal square on the door. I saw that when they got to it, the door opened, but I don't know what they did. We read the instructions from the disc carefully, and learned that we had to synchronize our eyes to a programme in the disc. Doing so, we are then capable of releasing sensitive light to the crystal panel, and then it will work. I said, "So that's it! Eye reflection! No wonder your lovely blue eyes capture me, now let's see what they can do to this space ship.." She smiled.

"You're awfully funny! But that's not going to get us anywhere. I'll try first!" She went up to the crystal square and looked at it - nothing happened - not a movement. "You've lost your touch," I said. "Let the brown-eyed one do his trick!"

"Go ahead," she said. "Beautiful brown eyes!"

I went and looked into the crystal panel, and nothing happened. "We must have read the instructions wrong," I said. "Let's go through them again, maybe, we missed something."

The instructions were clear. This sort of ship had this special entry through the light of the eyes. One must concentrate hard. "I will try again," Heidi said, and went up to the crystal square. She looked in, gazing, concentrating, and suddenly, the door slide apart, and we stepped in. We were in a small corridor, and we turned right and walked down it until we came to a door on the left. This too, had a crystal square. We had no trouble getting in for we knew now, what we had to do.

Everything looked as if it was brand new, just spectacular to look upon it. Just to the right of us is what we make to be the control area because it had two beautiful seats not far from each other. Panels and panels of push buttons, all different colors. We noticed as soon as we sat in the chairs, they operated automatically. Just to our left, high up and round, was what looked like a screen, underneath that was a standing panel filled with various buttons. Within this circular space we were in, we had never seen so many panels, and so many buttons. I was seated in the seat on the right, looking awestruck at the panel. Heidi took the seat on the left, and she too, couldn't believe her eyes, what they were seeing. On the panel before me were five rows of buttons, each row numbering 12. Below them were gauges with lines drawn from one to the other. High above these were six red buttons. To their left and right in groups of four were more graphs and buttons. But what caught our eyes was the panel with a round blue button, next to it a smaller one that was red. Then to the right of that 8 more buttons. The disc had told us what those buttons were for. In between a row of 12 buttons, there were 6 green buttons, three on one side and three on the other.

With instructions from the disc we pushed in certain buttons, and suddenly, the place came alive with strange noises, and there appeared before us a screen showing the outside.

I pushed in another button which the disc said would turn on the computer. We heard a voice at the side of us speaking. It asked for a code, and we gave the code. After that, we listened to information all about the ship, and where things were. Now we were beginning to settle in, and get acquainted with this new set up. Leaving the flight deck we went back out the door, turned left along the corridor and came to a flight of small stairs leading downwards. We took them and came to an area that was cordoned off with a sort of glassy fabric. This area was also circular. Then we saw in the middle what looked like a reddish/yellowish/bluish thing bubbling up in a sealed enclosure.

The computer had mentioned this area, but it hadn't told us what was going on. We were left clueless to what it was. Making our way back up, on the left of us was another door with a crystal square. We would check that out later. Back in the flight deck, we asked the computer what that stuff was that we saw below. It told us that that was the energy source. Strange, I thought.

Heidi asked the computer, "How far are we from earth?"

"20 light years."

"How long would it take us to get back to earth," I asked.

"Our ships are very fast, and can get you back in quick time. There are some ships that can change into light. Within the ship, time for you is very slow."

"Could you start the ship and let us see?" I asked the computer.

"That, I will do!"

There was a noise, a high pitched noise, at first, then everything was still. Looking at the screen, we realize, the ship had moved, and was now high up above, then it came back down to where it was.

Heidi said, "Thank you computer, we know quite a lot now!"

"At your service," the voice from the computer said.

"Tell me computer," I said, "are there faster ships than this one? And how much faster?"

"The ships from earth would take thousands of years to travel a few light years. We can do that without any problem. Our ships are made for that purpose, but we are not so advanced as those from other solar systems. They deal in particles of light, and break down space and time."

"Thanks for now,, computer," I said.

On one of the panels just at the side of Heidi, she spotted a dial that was tumbling over numbers. For a while, she looked at it, then she realized that there was something wrong. She said to me that the ship was ready to blow up any minute, showing me the dial. "It's just a counter," I told her.

"A counter for what?" She asked. "I don't like this at all! Let's get away from here!" She tried to get out her seat and found that the automatic release wasn't working. She was trapped in her seat. Then I saw clearly that we had ten minutes before the ship blew itself up. I quickly got the disc and began looking at the images for the seat. I saw that these seats can operate manually and automatically. Setting the manual release switch on, the silver looking belt released itself and Heidi was free.

"Let's get to hell out of here!" I told her, both hurrying to get to the main door. At the main door, I said, "Now you have to concentrate really good and get it right the first time."

Her blue eyes stared into the crystal square, and we waited and waited, the door stayed locked.

"What's wrong this time?" I said. "Keep looking into the crystal square."

With only five minutes left, the main door started opening, and we both got out safely, found our vehicle, and was out of the area. The blast of the ship went off exactly on time. There was no one around to get hurt. We stopped off at Michael, Cathy and Bernice's house. Hearing our story, Michael said, "Were you expecting to fly that ship?"

"I was going to give it a try," I told him. "With instructions from the disc, and the ship's main computer, it would have happened."

"That would have been splendid mum and dad if you had flown the ship!" Michael told us.

Cathy said, "We are so pleased that you're OK, and no harm came to you. It must have been very interesting to be in that ship, both of you alone!"

Heidi said, "It was a ship that was programmed to blow itself up, luckily, we escaped!"

I said, "They had crystal gadgets that worked with eye waves. They gave us a hard time. By the way, our space people would be arriving soon to give us a talk about the red star and our trip back to earth."

The space people came down with their ships. Our favorite commander was amongst them. We all gathered in the rest room, with Harold and Mary present. The commander told us what was going on. They had discovered a new energy, and was going to show us how it works. The first volunteer was Heidi. She got instructions to think of only outside, nothing else, concentrate on being outside. The rest of us were amazed, when suddenly, Heidi was outside, and waving back to us. Now that was something we never expected, The commander said, "That's how you're going to travel back to earth - through spiritual energy - and then change back again. You will all get the training you need. I said, "Wait a while commander! You're not serious, are you?"

"I am serious. It can be done, and you all are going to do it!"

"But... How can you get Bernice to do that?"

"There's no problem at all. She'll manage it. In that way you'll conquer time, and all those trillions of miles between you. Projecting yourself instantly from one place to the next,"

"Harold and Mary, wont it affect them? They're not young anymore!" I said.

"They too, will be able to do it," the commander said. "You'll find yourself back on earth, you'll change to your normal selves, and be doing what earth people do."

We found out that the earth had gone 9 years since we were away. The people who came up from the earth were not able to use this spiritual energy, for they were not told anything about it, and how it works. They will be transported to mother-ships, and because they had changed, just like us, when they first arrived, they would stay in space on mother-ships. Information came that the red star is about to flare up again, this time affecting the atmosphere on Nepsi. We were taken immediately away up to the space people's mother-ship. There in a beautiful room, we would practice more on spiritual energy, transporting the body to any place we should think of. It seemed to me here that we took on another body that was spiritual. I often wondered what happened to the old body. And how can we go on living again, when we should arrive back on the earth. But the space people knew all the answers. We were told that there's another body of light. It was a weird experience at first, but after a while, much practiced accomplished, it became very easy to us. There's no sense of time, no sense of physical being. Nothing seems real, only that you have this strange feeling of being. It took quite some time to get into that state, but it was not a physical state, and hard to describe.

The red star flared up and started expanding. We looked on from the mother-ship. This mother-ship wasn't as big as the first one we visited, but was a fair size. It was time for us now to depart, to journey back to earth with spiritual energy. The concentration started, the visualization of where we want to be, the breathing process.

There I was, in the farmer's field where the small space ships of the space people had always landed. There was Michael, Cathy, Mary, Harold, Bernice, and no Heidi. We waited patiently, and in five minutes thereabout, she appeared.

I said, "You had us worried then, for we would not know what to do if you had not turned up, and I hadn't the disc on me. Everyone is here. We all made it. This is just marvelous!"

Heidi said, "What happened to all those trillions of kilometers between the earth and where we were. What a mysterious journey?" She looked across, her house was still there.

Michael said, "So much I have to write in my book, some people are not going to believe that it really happened."

Harold said, "It's going to sound strange when we tell about such a journey, they would think that we were crazy. And how strange it was, so suddenly, and we are here."

Cathy said to Bernice, "Are you OK? Do you know what happened?"

Bernice answered, "I had to think very hard, and to keep seeing this farm field, always to keep it in my mind."

"We are back on earth again, fancy something nice to eat?"

I said. "I wonder what's on TV?"

First, we had to go to the offices which were still there, and pick up our keys. The earth was still in a terrible state, it had been damaged badly. The moon was still in its orbit around the earth.

It was the comet that did most damage to earth. The earth wasn't like it used to be before. The area where our house was hadn't been damaged, it was just the same as we had left it, a few cobwebs here and there. Heidi parents were a bit older, and so was the dog. It was glad to see us back again. We all decided to meet in my garden one day, and chat over our past experiences.

All the family were there in my garden on a nice sunny day. I started telling Heidi's parents about my experiences in space and how I felt. "Space," I told them, "was something out of this world. To see part of it with your own eyes is just great. Traveling in the ships where you don't feel any movement at all, and time slows down. The place we were was really nothing compare to the rest of space which is vast. Then our journey back with spiritual energy is an experience I shall never forget. It's just amazing, didn't seem real, and yet it was."

Not long after, Michael had his book published and it sold like mad. We heard that earth was planning a space expedition where they would live on mother-ships, and move from one solar system to the next, with no plans of coming back to earth. Earth got another scare from a comet that was heading for it, suddenly, it veered off. How lucky we were! Back in our routine, we visited holiday parks, and even took a trip to Paris. Over the years, the space people kept in touch with us. On one of their trips, I got a disc which was updated. Earth became more peaceful, and there weren't many wars amongst the nations.

The End

www.ingramcontent.com/pod-product-compliance
Lightning Source LLC
Chambersburg PA
CBHW020328130626
46549CB00003B/1070